CLIMATE CHANGE

A Novella

DANIEL DURRANT

Sirens Call Publications

Climate Change

CLIMATE CHANGE

Sirens Call Publications

ONE

"Phantom Street!" the driver bellowed, stopping the tram. "Last stop before the docks, ladies and gentlemen!"

Edward dallied whilst curiosity fought common sense. Delaying here posed a risk, but he thought a short visit would be safe enough. As a hiss of steam signaled the tram's departure, curiosity scored a knockout blow. He had to see.

He leapt down as the tram pulled away, his boots crumping into fresh snow.

"Shilling for a tour, sir?" an urchin offered, stepping into his path. "I know all the best ghosts, and you'll need no Medium to see them!"

Filthy children gathered behind the boy, forming up like a wolf pack. Although he knew far more than any guide could tell him, it seemed non-payment would buy trouble.

"I have no need of a tour," Edward said, flipping him the shilling. "But get yourself a decent meal, eh?" He moved on before they tried to repeat the tactic.

The street was fascinating. The positions of long-gone streetlamps were marked by permanent shadows on the wall. A ladder climbed a building two stories high, but existed only in silhouette. Then he saw the first phantom, unmistakably a woman. A few paces later he saw a child. They looked vaguely like life-size daguerreotypes, but each exposure was the remains of a living person, the developing agent the intense energy of the decay excursion. Vaporized in the blast, these indelible images were all that remained of them. It was as if their very souls had been burned into the masonry.

Sickened, he backed away.

"Don't move," a voice grated.

"I-" he began. The heavy *click* of a gun being cocked sounded behind him. *Those damned kids*, he thought. He felt a hand in his back pocket. "Take it," he said, unwilling to risk death over a few pounds.

"Give it back."

"Eh?" Edward turned to find a teenage boy holding his wallet in one hand, and a knife in the other. Behind him, a figure wrapped in furs held a revolver to his head.

Very slowly, the boy passed the money back.

"Go." A wave of the pistol reinforced the command.

The boy nodded, and ran. He disappeared into an alley.

"Sir, my sincere thanks." Edward ducked, trying to make eye contact under the hood, but a gas mask blocked his view. The stranger looked like a scout, perhaps in the employ of the Hudson's Bay Company. "If you had not-"

"Sir?" his savior repeated. "Do I really smell that bad?"

The stranger pulled back the hood, revealing long blonde hair tied back in a ponytail. The mask came off next. Underneath was one of the most beautiful women Edward had ever seen. He opened his mouth, but closed it again without speaking.

"Are you alright?"

Her English was perfect, but laced with an odd accent. She certainly wasn't local, though; no one here was blessed with the vivid health evidenced by her flawless complexion.

"Ah – we should move on," Edward stumbled. "This is no place for a lady."

"I see chauvinism manages to flourish even in the harsh climate of the frontier."

"Chauvinism? No, you misunderstand, madam. I meant not the street, but the whole town. Badash isn't safe for ladies. The enervating remnant, you know. I'm concerned for your constitution, not female sensibilities."

"You sound like a doctor."

"Indeed, although one of engineering. Doctor Edward Rankine. I should say at your service, but it seems to be the other way around." *God, she's beautiful*. As he recovered, instinct asserted itself. Try to be charming, it said. He couldn't walk away without her name, at least. "And who may I thank for my rescue?"

"I'm Charlotte. My friends call me Charlie."

"Charlotte," he repeated, reveling in the familiarity of her first name. "Well, if I may presume – Charlie, then I-"

A series of horn blasts echoed across town. Even a mile away from the docks, they were loud enough for the Royal Navy signal to be distinct.

"The *Dominator*," he groaned, looking at his watch. "She's preparing to leave. I have to go."

"Then perhaps you could escort me. For my safety," she added, with a sly smile.

"You have passage booked?" Edward tried not to show his surprise. *How can someone of the working class afford that?*

"My father arranged it," she said, setting off.

"So what brings you into town?" The question was an irrelevance; he just wanted an excuse to talk with her.

"Oh, a business venture. We can cut through here, I think," she said, leading him down a narrow alley.

It delivered them into a chaotic marketplace. It contained hundreds of stalls, but there had been no discernible attempt to set them out to any kind of plan.

"This way," she yelled, heading into the labyrinth.

The array of goods was bewildering. There was food of every kind, some of it still alive. Traders hawked everything from household supplies to spare machine parts. Artisans offered repairs. The next few stalls were curtained-off, and Edward was mystified as to their function until he heard the noises that came forth. *They supply a different kind of service altogether*, he thought.

"I wouldn't touch those," he cautioned, as Charlotte eyed a vendor offering grilled sausages. "Everything is tainted."

"Still?"

"And for many years to come. Eat after you board."

"The snow is the only clean thing here," she muttered, moving on.

It was literally true. Aside from the few surviving buildings on Phantom Street, Badash was new, built on the ruins of York Factory. The town had yet to see its tenth birthday, but seemed decrepit already. Dysfunction was everywhere, extending even into the cells of plants and animals. *Including the people,* he thought, looking at a deformed child. Realizing Charlotte had pushed on, he gave chase.

Another alleyway led down to the harbor. Dockers toiled, loading boats, but none of the ship's tenders were present.

"Come on!" he shouted, running for the pulley railway. Asking for a pier number was superfluous; the battle-cruiser occupied the entire length of the harbor's main jetty.

On the ride out, Edward tried to glimpse the modifications that were his design. All space forward was taken by three quadruple turrets. They began to pass the castle, but before the stern became visible, the ship was lost in a fog bank of her own making.

"She has decay engines?" Charlotte asked, watching steam engulf the superstructure.

"Yes, four." He pointed at the cooling towers. "I can arrange a tour if you'd like," he offered, hoping to impress.

"Yes." She smiled. "I would."

After hopping off at the loading pavilion, they pushed through the crowd and showed their papers to the Royal Marine manning the embarkation point. He directed them toward the nearest elevator, but as they approached, an enormous man began to close the gate.

"Hold, if you please!" Edward called, hurrying forward.

The giant hesitated, but dropped the latch at the signal of an expensively dressed woman standing beside him. The platform began to climb, but those aboard were unprepared. Near the guardrail, two men struggling with a huge portmanteau overbalanced.

Muscles battled gravity as the platform continued skyward. Gravity won. The luggage teetered on the edge before plummeting down, dragging one of the men behind it. They landed together. Clothes, trinkets, and blood dispersed across the unforgiving stone.

"Medic!" Charlotte yelled, running forward. "We need a doctor!"

Edward knelt down and grabbed the man's wrist, but found no pulse.

"We shan't need one, I'm afraid." He shook his head.

"He's dead?"

"Don't trouble yourself, Miss," a marine said. "He's only a Jack."

"A Jack?" Edward removed the man's woolen hat. The scalp beneath was fashioned not from flesh, but metal. A bundle of wires trailed down under his collar. He stood, and looked around. Free from distraction, it was obvious; the stevedores moved with the stilted gait of the converted.

"You bloody fools!" The woman from the elevator barged past them, directing her staff to clean up. "Don't touch that!" she shouted, as a maid picked up an ornate music box. She snatched the item away, and passed it to the tall man.

"Can I be of assistance?" Edward offered.

"I very much doubt it!" His offer seemed to feed her anger, but then she calmed. "It was a gift from my father," she said, perhaps trying to justify her outburst. "Excuse us."

"Lady Holden," Charlotte murmured, as they climbed aboard another elevator. "I see she's every bit as charming as her reputation suggests."

The name seemed familiar, but Edward had no chance to enquire about it.

As they stepped aboard, a young man burst through a service door, charging toward them.

"Stop!" someone hollered, but the man paid no heed. He dashed for a loading ramp, but a gunshot ended his journey. He collapsed beside them, blood erupting from his chest.

Marines ran forward with guns drawn, but had no more targets.

"Sir? Madam? Are you alright?" An officer lowered his weapon, and stepped forward.

Edward looked at the would-be escapee. Blood spread unchecked until it hit the edge of the plank under him. Acting like a miniature dyke, the caulking carried it to the gunwale drain.

"Yes, we're fine. Thank you, Lieutenant," Charlotte replied.

A rhythmic hammering sound finally drew Edward's attention from the body. Looking up, he saw Captain Fitzjames approaching. Standing nearly seven feet tall on his pneumatic legs, he strode forward to join them.

"I must apologize," the Captain said. "Hardly an appropriate welcome, Miss Redpath." He smiled. "It's a pleasure to see you again."

"Captain." She nodded. "I was most grieved to hear of your injury at the battle of Buenos Aires."

Redpath? Charlotte Redpath? Edward tried hard to keep his face blank, but knew he'd failed. Charlie? Stunned, he shook his head.

"Chance hit from a shore battery, but the objective was achieved. The Argentine Navy was completely destroyed." Shrugging, he tapped the brass thigh tank. "The admiralty insists my uniform should be tailored to hide them, but I believe it does the men good to see that officers share the danger with them." He turned to Edward. "Doctor Rankine, I presume?"

"Yes, Captain." As a civilian, Edward had no protocol to observe, but pulled himself upright nonetheless. "It's an honor, sir."

"Hmn. Frankly, I don't care for what you've done to my ship, Doctor. The loss of the aft turret concerns me." He frowned, but then a narrow smile crossed his lips. "However, I must admit I'm curious to see the system in action."

"Sir, look at this." Kneeling beside the body, a Marine pulled the man's shirt open. A small tree was tattooed on his sternum.

"Creationist!" Fitzjames growled. Air hissed from a bleed valve as he stamped a foot. "Lieutenant, organize a search-"

"Sir, we have another one!" Two Marines exited from the nearest elevator, dragging a man between them. "Caught him in the engine room, sir. Chief Engineer said he was tampering with the vortex transducers."

"You are aboard a vessel of the Royal Navy," Fitzjames said, clipping off each word. "Sabotaging a ship-of-the-line carries a mandatory life sentence. Take him for marionisation."

"No!" The man sagged down between his captors. Only their grip prevented his collapse. "Captain, I beg you!"

"I'm sorry, son. It's too late for that." He hesitated. "Be grateful we have a good surgeon. It won't hurt."

Listening to him scream as the Marines hauled him away, Edward wondered if the dead man hadn't been the luckier one. At least he couldn't suffer any more.

"Captain, chance seems an unlikely explanation for this," he said, trying to focus. "We have to consider that someone has leaked details of our mission."

"You're suggesting there's a traitor aboard the *Dominator*?" Fitzjames snarled.

Thinking himself the target of the Captain's anger, Edward took a step back.

"Damn it, you're right. Too much coincidence." He called the officers close. Through clenched teeth, he ordered an immediate departure. "We don't want a panic. Keep this quiet, but place double guards on all restricted areas." Surrounded by his entourage, he walked away, still issuing orders.

"You're Charlotte Redpath?" Edward asked.

"The last time I checked, yes." She looked down at herself.

"You might have told me." The daughter of one of the wealthiest industrialists in the world, and he'd taken her for some grubby scout. Edward shook his head, feeling dizzy. He couldn't take much more of this. As if the expedition alone wasn't terror enough, trouble had struck before the ship could even sail.

"I'm sorry, Edward." She touched his arm. "Don't sulk. It wouldn't have been nearly so much fun."

"Oh, Miss Redpath?" Fitzjames turned back. "As I said, this is a vessel of the Royal Navy." He gestured at her filthy clothes. "Sponsor or not, Her Majesty's rules dictate a dress code."

TWO

"Of course the Barbary pirates remain a problem, even after we destroyed Tripoli," Fitzjames said, concluding his latest tale. Like all naval officers, he seemed to hold an endless reserve. "They're like rats in the Orlop. You never get them all."

Edward nodded, but said nothing. Instead, he savored both his wine and the surroundings. Since he didn't imagine an engineer – executive or otherwise – would dine at the Captain's table very often, he was determined to enjoy it.

"Tell me, Captain, is it really true they sell those captured into slavery?" a woman asked. Her face was covered by a thick mask of cosmetic emollient. Presumably she thought it could hide her age.

"I'm afraid so, yes. Many are auctioned off in the Turkish bazaars, although the Ottomans deny it."

"Even the women? How positively ghastly." She pulled a face, but was clearly thrilled by the horror of it.

"Well, I'm sure we're quite safe here. No corsair would survive an encounter with the *Dominator*, eh, Captain?" Rupert said.

The eldest son of the Duke of Suffolk, his prodigious energy and wealth were apparently focused solely on the pursuit of fun. Despite his obvious intelligence, he took nothing seriously. In short, he was everything Edward hated, yet it seemed impossible not to like him. There was something infectious in his manner.

"But let's not talk of ugly things in the presence of such beauty." Grinning, Rupert pushed back his chair, and got to his feet.

Confused by the remark, Edward belatedly realized a lady was approaching. He leapt up, not wishing to appear uncouth. Charlotte had arrived. Scrubbed clean, and squeezed into an evening gown, she was scarcely recognizable. She was loveliness defined, yet somehow, he preferred the woman he'd met in Badash. Perhaps it was simply because they'd been alone. There, he'd not had to share her with anyone. His mood lifted on discovering she was to occupy the empty seat to his right.

"You needn't stop on my account," she said, sitting. "I hear that if the Ottomans continue their triangle trade, Parliament may target Constantinople."

"Well informed, as always, Miss Redpath." Fitzjames beckoned the waiting staff forward.

A moment later, chimes rang, broadcast over the ship's ampliphone system. They sounded pleasantly melodious, but were orders, not entertainment. Responding to the prompt, the marionettes switched tasks and began to assist. Dinner was served.

"Capital! I shall reserve tickets as soon as possible," Rupert said, thumping the table. "I'd like to see the brutes get what they deserve."

"Turks have the right idea if you ask me," slurred the Earl of Warwick. He waved an unsteady hand at the Jacks clearing a table nearby. "The puppets are no substitute for the real thing. Damned abolitionists have cost the Empire its greatest resource."

Cutlery clattered on porcelain whilst safe replies were considered.

"I'm not sure Miss Holden would agree," Rupert ventured. "What do you say, Natalie?"

Hearing the two names together, Edward finally made the connection. Holden Resources. A gifted inventor, her father had patented the marionisation process, amongst other things.

"The product is not yet perfect, of course," she replied, setting down her fork. "The early models could handle only five tasks. But we continue to make rapid progress. These are Jack-Nines." She pointed at a serving maid. "And those are Jill-Twelves."

"Why the difference?" Edward asked, unable to suppress his curiosity.

"The women multi-task better. Just as in life." She looked around the table as if expecting support, but the other ladies avoided comment. If she'd been expecting female solidarity from Charlotte, she'd been badly mistaken.

"Is that how you see them – as product?" Charlotte asked, a scarcely-concealed edge on her voice.

"Any life-sentence crime renders them state property. Property which we legally purchase," Natalie replied. It was well rehearsed, the manner of someone used to deflecting attacks. "So, yes, that is precisely what they are."

"Well, I think it's very clever," the Earl's young wife said. "It's like that idea I read about in the paper. You know, how you make something useful from waste." She nudged her husband. "What was it, dear?"

"Eh? Oh – recycling?"

"That's it. What else can we do, with so many criminals throughout the Empire?"

"Yes, it is amazing how many crimes are committed in the colonies," Charlotte replied, with heavy sarcasm.

Edward's normally rapid mind was being slowed by alcohol, and he failed to grasp her meaning until he looked around the dining room. Whilst there were Jacks and Jills of every race, they were overwhelmingly foreign. Very few faces were white. Feeling hopelessly naïve, he stopped drinking. *Has my life been so sheltered?*

"We make best use of the resource," Holden countered.

"There are other methods."

"Methods such as your father's?" she sneered. "Giving away profit to your workers?"

"Surely not?" the made-up woman gasped. She'd looked less appalled by news of the slave markets.

"My father's companies run as co-operatives," Charlotte replied. "Employees," she said, emphasizing the word, "are given shares. If the company does well, the shares pay a dividend. Thus, staff are well-motivated."

"And this works?" she asked.

"Extremely well, if the operation in Kenya is an example," Rupert said. "I visited the Safari Park last year. I hear you thought of it."

He was aiming to charm, Edward realized. Annoyed, he tried to think of something clever to say, but nothing presented itself.

"Yes. Commercial farming of the large game animals reduces costs, and ensures a steady supply of both meat and ivory. And we collect hunting fees instead of paying slaughter men – a double saving."

"Ingenious." Flattery complete, Rupert steered the conversation back into safer territory. "So, Captain, tell us about your new command. I understand we're aboard the first true Battle-cruiser?"

"Indeed. Although not the first chimera – the *Colonial* class battleship HMS *Cathay* had luxury accommodation added some years ago – the *Dominator* was the first capital ship with cruise amenities designed-in. The first century ship to be equipped as such, too."

"Over a hundred thousand tons," Edward explained, noticing Charlotte's frown.

"One hundred and seven thousand long tons, to be precise," Fitzjames said, with manifest enthusiasm. "Until the new *Victoria* class super-dreadnoughts are commissioned, we're the largest ship extant."

"She is remarkable," Edward agreed, glancing at the plasmascope that displayed their course and speed. Easing the ship through the labyrinth of whale cages that filled Hudson Bay had made for slow progress, but in the Strait, they were free to use maximum power. The ship was averaging a scarcely believable thirty-nine knots. They would reach the Labrador Sea before the day was out.

"Madam," boomed someone close behind him.

Reflex took him halfway to his feet before he was able to check the move. Settling back down, he found Holden's giant manservant had appeared.

"Samuel, prepare my quarters." She pressed a button on what Edward had first assumed to be a cigarette case. "Turn up the heating. And set up my music box – I should like to listen for a little while."

He nodded once, and set off.

"He's a marionette?" Edward asked, as she put the device away. "I had no idea they could talk."

"Samuel is a prototype. He's state of the art. We have him up to seventeen tasks now." She smiled. "If you'll all excuse me, I'm rather tired. I think I shall retire early."

Following Fitzjames' example, the men stood until her back was turned.

"Hmn? Yes, please," Rupert said, as a waitress arrived bearing a silver service.

The girl began to pour his coffee. She missed the cup, but continued regardless. The dark liquid flooded across the tablecloth.

"Manipulator!" Fitzjames bellowed.

A crewman rushed across. He pointed a control rod at the girl, but to no avail.

She continued until the pot was empty. Looking confused, she dropped it. She staggered away, but made only a few paces before collapsing to the floor, blood pouring from her nose.

"Breakdown," Charlotte whispered.

The girl rolled back and forth, thrashing like a fish out of water. She growled something incomprehensible through a jaw locked tight by seizure. Then, foaming at the mouth, she stopped moving. A stain spread down the back of her uniform as her bowels emptied.

A vast woman in a bustle gown began screaming. Then she fainted.

"Good Lord!" Rupert said, rising. "Edward, help me, eh? Let's get the poor lady outside."

Edward hesitated, trying to find the least improper way of taking her weight. In the end, physics overrode etiquette; holding her shoulders, they escorted her away like two men supporting a drunken friend.

"Well, there you have it. No substitute," the Earl of Warwick crowed, as they staggered toward the door. "Just like I said."

THREE

When the commotion settled, Edward returned to look for Charlotte, but she had vanished. Only Rupert was to be found, smoking on the promenade deck.

"Oh, hello, Edward. No early night for you, then?"

"No, I shall try to get some work done." He gestured back toward the lounge. "Poor Miss Holden seems to be rather stressed." He lit a cigar of his own. "If the polar extremes trouble her, I really don't know why she came."

"Women generally prefer the comfort of civilization," Rupert agreed, "but in this case I fear you've hit the nail already – 'poor' being the word under the hammer, so to speak. This might well be her last cruise."

"Poor?" he echoed. "Surely not! Through the patent, Holden Resources has an effective monopoly on the conversion trade. Her wealth must be unimaginable!"

"Not anymore." Rupert tapped ash over the side. "Bad investments, you know. Her father paid a fortune for prospecting rights in Persia, and do you know what he found? Nothing but oil, and they're struggling to extract it anyway."

"That should be simple enough. It's filthy stuff, but easy to tap."

"I shall bow to your expertise there, but I believe the problem is political, rather than technical. The natives keep sabotaging the wells – you wouldn't believe the amount of heavy equipment they've had to send out there. They even started attacking the engineers. From what I've heard, they don't fear death one jot. Which is fortunate," he added.

"Meaning?"

"A friend of mine touring the Gulf visited Bushehr." He lowered his voice. "Said the place was depopulated, practically a ghost town. Rumor says it got so bad that the Middle East Company authorized a germ strike. Jenner bombs, probably."

"It's happened before." Edward shivered. He knew the Empire had such weapons available – there could be typhoid shells aboard the *Dominator* right now – but preferred not to think about it. "I don't suppose Miss Redpath is still around?"

"Edward, you're a fine fellow, but too earnest by half," Rupert said, misinterpreting his interest as professional. He tossed his cigar over the side. "There's plenty of time to prepare for your project."

"Perhaps not." He watched the stub tumble down into water no longer entirely liquid. The sea was now topped with a thick slush he'd heard the crew call 'frazil ice'. "Even at this latitude, the sea is freezing."

"Relax a little, old man! We've scarcely seen you out of your mysterious shed since we left port." Rupert punched his shoulder. "You know what you need? A little late night drink. My treat." He pulled Edward into the elevator. After extracting a first class key from his pocket, he unlocked a panel above the floor buttons. Behind lay an additional button, but it bore no number.

"Where are we going?" Edward asked, as the elevator began to climb.

"Deck thirteen – the Crow's Club. Lucky for some!" he cackled.

The motors whirred away for another thirty seconds before the doors opened. They emerged into an observation lounge, but the windows displayed only the solid curtain of night. Venturing closer to the glass, Edward saw the lamps of the promenade deck lay two hundred feet below. They were actually higher than the bridge; the suite must occupy the enclosed section of the Tesla tower, he reasoned. Only the array itself was higher than this room.

Responding to Rupert's call, Edward followed him into the parlor. It took a moment for his eyes to adjust. In the dim light, men reclined on couches, drinking. Some drew on ornate hookahs, filling the air with a rich smoke.

At the center of the room, two dancing girls writhed around poles. Edward imagined their outfits to be impossibly tight before realizing the truth. Completely nude, they wore only paint.

"Excuse me." Rupert beckoned a waitress. "Table for two – in the back."

"Yes, sir."

"Good God," Edward choked, watching her walk away. The drinks tray seemed to cover more of her modesty than the miniscule lace garments she wore.

"This is but the entree," Rupert said, following her through a door. "The finest of everything from all four corners of the Empire flows to this very spot."

He pulled Edward into a scene woven from the fabric of dreams, or perhaps nightmares. It might have been both.

A maze formed of velvet partitions held women representing every imaginable aspect of humanity. Europeans were present, some blonde, and some brunette. Behind a too-thin chiffon curtain, a redhead straddled a man. A dozen girls wearing no more than silk scarves represented the East Indies. An African woman – Ashanti, Edward thought – wore her tribal jewelry and nothing else. Two girls wrapped in tiny ribbons of wolf pelt looked Esquimaux. They disappeared behind another curtain with a hugely obese man.

"This place is –" He trailed off, too shocked to finish.

"Remarkable, isn't it? Here, sit." Rupert beckoned another waitress to the booth, and ordered drinks. "These are a nice touch," he said, lighting a fresh cigar on the table lamp. "Gas is just – I don't know – more romantic, don't you think? Can't abide the cold glare of those electric jobs."

"It's because of the engines," Edward murmured, still looking at the women. Romance as a concept seemed not to belong in here. "The seawater passing through the decay sanctum is cracked into its constituent parts," he explained, retreating into the comfort zone of science. "We get hydrogen and oxygen as by-products. No sense in wasting them, hence the gas lamps."

"Edward, for God's sake! Switch that mighty brain of yours off. How can you think of engineering in here? Interesting, though," he allowed. "I never knew that."

A girl wearing a tiger fur swished past. Complete with head and tail, the skin had been fashioned into a body suit, but one that left her breasts and private parts exposed.

"Ah, something finally holds your attention," Rupert said, following his gaze. "Yes, we even have own menagerie." He passed over a glass. "Cheers!"

Still staring, Edward took a huge gulp. The absinthe burned, but the sensation seemed distant.

"She's impressive, alright," Rupert agreed. He waved at a man behind the bar. "But allow me to recommend something from the menu."

Two Chinese girls approached. Already naked, they carried a silver tray between them. They knelt down, and began loading opium pipes.

"Uh, Rupert," Edward began, "I don't really-"

"Oh, live a little. This is the best stuff, direct from Guangzhou. Won't do you any harm."

When the pipes were ready, one of the girls lit a small oil lamp.

Edward considered refusal, but since he was unable to conceive a graceful way out, he took the pipe. Copying Rupert, he warmed the bowl over the flame before inhaling. Despite his shallow breath, the vapor intoxicated him immediately; it was like a dozen drinks all at once.

"That's amazing," he slurred.

"It gets better." Rupert pointed at the girls.

Working together, they mixed ingredients in a glass bowl. Edward watched them arrange paraphernalia on the tray. Their movements were so concise and well-practiced that they seemed almost mechanical. An awful thought occurred.

"Are they marionettes?"

"Good God, man, of course not! You'd think I'd trust some Jill with my equipment? She blows a valve at the wrong moment and I'll have no heir! No, these are corvées. Since the Emperor was unable to meet the last opium tithe, some girls were provided as part of the shipment." He grinned. "Although I hear some do have a fancy for the automata."

"That's revolting!"

"Apparently the latest prototypes have new abilities." He raised an eyebrow. "Rumor has it that Samuel's seventeenth task is quite demanding." He giggled. "Perhaps that's why she looks frustrated all the time!"

"You can't be serious." Edward sat upright again.

"Stranger things happen," he said. "But for now, let's focus on the mysteries of the Orient."

The girls decanted viscous syrup into small cups. It looked like treacle, but Edward was just together enough to realize the dark color came from alkaloids, not sugar.

Together, the girls drained the cups, working the fluid around their lips.

"We have the infernal stuff in such quantity that even the meretrices are allowed it?" Edward gasped.

"Not quite, my friend." Rupert smiled. "It's not for their benefit."

Edward failed to understand until one of the girls knelt before Rupert. A part of his brain said that he was supposed to object, that this was all wrong, but other voices spoke louder. He drew on the pipe again as the other girl approached him.

A reindeer walked past on all fours. The creature turned toward him. Edward tried to focus. It looked disturbingly real, but there had to be a girl inside. He sought eye contact, but was unable to decide if a woman looked out from beneath the antlers or not.

Overwhelmed, Edward surrendered. He slumped back, adrift on a sea of sensation.

FOUR

Edward's heart raced as another tremor passed through the deck. He ignored it, and focused on his work. The device was ready. He checked the connections once more, and then replaced the inspection plate.

Intellectually, he understood the ship had been designed with polar operations in mind, and was thus well up to the task of pushing through the Arctic ice. Instinct, however, argued differently. Ice scraping along the hull sounded far too much like buckling metal.

A tremendous shrieking noise travelled from bow to stern. In his mind, another row of rivets popped out. He sat down, and began to massage his temples. Last night's adventures were still costing him dear. His memory was fragmented at best, but his overall impression was that someone must have mugged him. Nothing less could cause such a terrible headache.

"Good afternoon." Charlotte appeared in the doorway. "Am I finally allowed into your lair?"

"Yes, yes, of course." He managed to rise, but doing so amplified the headache further. Feeling dizzy, he sat again. "The Captain only wanted the area off-limits until we were away from civilization."

"So this is the secret." She stepped inside. "And I can see why," she gasped, studying the equipment. "It looks like we're ready for war, not exploration."

Her remark was apt. The space previously occupied by the turret barbette now held four vast discharge racks. Each ran down to a ramp inside the stern doors. The rows of decay capacitrons awaiting launch looked more like naval mines than any instrument of science.

Watching her look around, Edward was aware he was missing an obvious opportunity to impress her, or at least show off, but he felt too ill to deliver.

"Well, it's nice to have some company," he tried. "It's been lonely down here."

"Oh, my poor Edward," she cooed. "Have you been allowed no visitors at all?"

"No." Her choice of words made him feel somewhat better. "Even the Captain has stayed away, despite his alleged interest."

"Well, he has mixed feelings about this whole thing. Inevitable, I suppose."

"Why?"

"You don't know?" She raised an eyebrow. "Naval service is a tradition in his family. His grandfather was killed on a previous attempt to traverse the passage. Well, I say killed. Technically missing, but presumed dead," she corrected.

"Fitzjames," Edward breathed. "Of course – he was commander of the *Erebus*!" His knowledge of history was limited, but it was impossible to be British and not know the story of the Franklin expedition. Although their exact fate remained unknown, investigators believed the ships had become icebound somewhere in Victoria Strait. "The poor souls all died."

"So they say." She sat down. "Me, I'm not so sure. When I travelled in the Northwest Territories, I met tribal elders that had seen white people before. *Kabloona*, they called them. They claimed the men had walked overland from Qikiqtaq – that's King William Land, to you and I."

"Surely not," he objected. "That's hundreds of miles."

"They found bodies, too. They say the flesh had been stripped from the bones." She hesitated. "I wonder if they might have survived by eating their companions as they fell – Edward?" She looked at him. "Are you alright?"

"Quite alright, thank you." He wasn't. He'd felt bad enough before her story. Now, the urge to vomit was overwhelming.

"Have you eaten? I missed you at breakfast."

"Yes, yes," he lied. "Very busy day, you know."

"You missed lunch too. Are you sure you're alright?" She frowned. "You don't look at all well. Is it seasickness, perhaps?"

"No!" he protested, unwilling to appear weak. "Of course not. I think that – something may have disagreed with me."

"I heard you went to the Crow's Club."

"Ah – yes," he admitted. She was playing with him, then. "Rupert invited me." He offered a silent prayer. Surely the women wouldn't know what went on up there?

"I see."

Inside, Edward cursed expansively. "You needn't look at me like that," he said. "I simply went for a late drink."

"Right."

"It's true, I swear!"

It was true. Nothing had happened, although his virtue had been saved by physical weakness rather than moral strength. He'd passed out under the opium. God willing, Rupert would stay quiet.

"Well, you're under a lot of pressure," she said, looking around the room. "I suppose you should try to relax. You know, Inuit women have a saying." She rattled off something he couldn't understand. "It means, 'a man with full balls cannot think'. You need to concentrate, after all."

"Charlotte!" Edward felt warmth spread across his face.

"Sorry. Have I embarrassed you? I may have spent too much time amongst the Esquimaux. They're very open about all that, you know. They see it as natural, and nothing to be ashamed of."

"I really didn't do anything."

"Alright, Edward." She smiled. "I believe you."

"So what were you doing with the Esquimaux, anyway?" he asked, seizing the chance to divert the conversation.

"My father has a new venture in the region." Her smile suggested she recognized his maneuver, but she let it go. "The area contains precious metals, possibly even diamonds. That's his interest in this – if the passage can be forged, the open trade route would be of enormous benefit. The Esquimaux are uniquely qualified to operate in the environment. We hope to form a partnership with the Yellowknife tribes." She nodded at the machinery. "Edward, this scheme of yours, can it really work?"

"According to Lord Kelvin's calculations, yes." Relieved to be back on safe ground, he tapped the nearest device. "Each capacitron is effectively a miniature version of the *Dominator's* engines – a kind of decay battery, if you will. Once activated, the isentropic crucible reaches incredible temperatures. With-"

"Sir!" Maxwell, one of his deputy engineers, burst out of the control room. "Bridge reports pack ice ahead. This is it!"

"Already?" Edward looked at the huge chart pinned to the wall. He'd hoped to reach Barrow Strait before deploying the first device. "Damn. Prepare for release!"

Staff flooded in. Assisted by the Jacks Captain Fitzjames had assigned him, Edward's team readied the system. The launch ramp was moved into position.

He climbed up to the first device and grabbed the arming key. It all came down to this. Murmuring another brief prayer to a God he didn't believe in, Edward pulled the safety device out. A clunk from inside confirmed the fuel had released. He jumped down and placed a hand against the ceramic shell. After a few seconds, it began to warm.

"Good luck, old man!"

Edward turned to find Rupert at the head of a crowd, come to bear witness. He supposed it was an appropriately historic moment, but he could have done without the distraction.

"Brace yourselves!" shouted another engineer. He yanked the lever to open the stern doors.

Charlotte fastened her fur coat as Arctic winds blasted through the bay.

Venturing as close to the ramp as he dared, Edward looked down at the icy waters beneath.

"Go!" He signaled for release.

The capacitron stuck on the cold iron for an instant. Then, groaning, it rolled forward and left the ramp. He watched it splash into the icy water. The heavy device sank almost instantly.

As the doors closed, Edward marked their position on the chart. "Prepare DC-two," he ordered, calculating the distance. They had only a few minutes.

"Here's to the Northwest Passage!" a man yelled. He sounded drunk already, but the crowd apparently liked the sentiment. Cheering broke out.

"Congratulations," Charlotte said. Stepping close to him, she lowered her voice. "Edward, will it work? Truly? Can even-" She looked at the racks for a moment. "One hundred and ninety-two of the things really conquer this environment?"

"Conquer? No. But we need only make a small difference. With enough devices in place, the water temperature will rise – only by a few degrees – but enough, Charlie. Enough to guarantee free shipping for three months in summer, and ice-breaker access for perhaps two months on either side."

"Well done!" Rupert said. The crowd came with him, ending their moment of intimacy. Annoyed at the intrusion, Edward submitted to the round of handshakes.

"They get that hot?" she asked, ignoring the interlopers.

"The victorium three-oh-five core burns hotter than the sun itself."

"Three-oh-five?" she repeated. "I thought imperium two-ninety-one occupied the highest periodic position."

"Well, in a sense it still does." He didn't want to spoil the moment by correcting her. "Victorium doesn't actually occur in nature. We have to produce it by refining imperium."

"Fascinating." She caught his eye. "So, once again, Mr. Mendeleev needs to set more places at his table."

His smile took a moment to arrive; Edward doubted anyone had fashioned a witticism from the elements of the periodic table before. Moreover, there was almost no chance anyone else present would understand. Her joke was private, intended for him only. His smile widened as he turned back to the group.

"Sir, second launch?" Maxwell prompted.

"Yes, indeed." Allowing his deputy to take the lead, Edward stepped back and watched them make the next device ready.

After checking the ramp, Maxwell climbed up to remove the key.

"All clear!" he yelled, grabbing the release lever.

As the crew moved away from the ramp, Edward saw one of the Jacks freeze. Something was wrong with it. He started forward, but the marionette seemed to recover.

It moved away from the doors, but instead of following the group, it veered left, staggering toward Maxwell.

Edward heard Rupert shout a warning, but it came too late.

The Jack lunged forward, and grabbed Maxwell's arm. Then it stepped onto the ramp, dragging the engineer behind.

Trying to break free, Maxwell sought something to grab onto. His free arm found the release lever. As they fell onto the rails, he tripped the launch.

The capacitron rolled forward, gathering speed. It hit the ramp, but the engineer's body lay across the starboard rail.

Edward had no plan, but instinct drove him forward nonetheless. Moving closer afforded him an excellent view of Maxwell's death. His chest was crushed as the seventeen-ton device passed over him. Then the capacitron hit the Jack. Slowed by the first impact, it stopped, the body forming a human chock on the rails.

No one spoke for several seconds. Then the screaming started.

"Help me!" Edward yelled, grabbing Rupert.

"He's dead, man! Show some respect."

"No!" Respect could come later. "We have to release it. Now!"

First to understand his urgency were the engineers. As one, they leapt forward and began trying to drag the Jack free.

They needed leverage. Edward grabbed a pry bar from the bench, and tried to alleviate the pressure. The Jack howled. His first thought was that he'd wounded the creature. Then he smelled burning flesh. The core was active. It was being cooked alive.

"Edward, calm down-" Rupert began.

"You don't understand! The device relies on immersion to cool it – in the air, it'll overload. The excursion will destroy the whole ship!"

"Then turn the damn thing off!"

"I can't!"

The crew continued wrestling with the Jack, but they struggled to keep hold of him. Agony drove the creature to thrash around, breaking their grasp.

"For God's sake!" Charlotte shouted. "He's already dead! Put the poor thing-" Swearing, she ran across the bay and grabbed a revolver from the arms locker. She strode back, shoved past the engineers, and fired a single shot to the head.

With the body still, and extra pry bars levering the capacitron back, they were finally able to pull the ruined Jack free.

The device rolled down the ramp. As it struck the sea, ice went from solid to liquid to gas in an instant. An enormous plume of steam rose skywards. The surface churned with bubbles after the capacitron vanished, boiling the sea as it sank.

Chest heaving, Edward retreated from the ramp and closed the doors. If it had been much longer... He pushed the thought away.

"What happened?" Charlotte asked, still holding the revolver.

"I don't know." He looked at Maxwell. What on earth could have prompted such an attack? "It must be a malfunction of some kind."

"Or the work of more creationists," Rupert suggested, straightening his suit.

"Perhaps." Edward summoned his staff. "Get this cleaned up. We have to be ready for launch three."

Trying to ignore the smell, he set about examining the Jack. The body was wrecked; he could learn nothing there. He looked at the head. The man looked familiar. Recognizing the face, Edward recoiled. Between the skull implants and the gunshot wound, the head was badly damaged, but it was definitely him. It was the saboteur captured as they'd come aboard.

DANIEL DURRANT

FIVE

As a boy, Edward had read Mary Shelley's novel *Frankenstein*. Over the years, he'd come to imagine a Marionisation lab might look something like the eponymous scientist's laboratory, but it didn't. It was far, far worse.

On entry, Edward found a Jack laid out on a table. The top of his head had been removed, exposing the brain beneath. Unhelpfully, his mind likened it to the hardboiled egg he'd cracked open at breakfast. Feeling sick, he moved on.

A Jill occupied the next spot. She was naked. Slim, she had been pretty in life, but there was nothing sexual in the scene. Implants protruded from her skull. A huge incision crossed her abdomen. It was no more erotic than a side of meat on a butcher's slab.

Staying well clear of the bodies, he went through to the operating theater. A man was busy removing implants from another Jack. The crushed saboteur, in fact.

"Doctor Lister?"

"Hmn?" he replied, without looking up.

Edward cringed as the doctor withdrew a glass cylinder from the cranium. For that to fit inside, a huge chunk of brain must have been removed.

"I was hoping we could talk for a moment. I'm Edward Rankine."

"Ah! Pleased to meet you." He began to offer his hand, looked at the blood soaked glove, and retracted it. "Shan't shake, then. I trust your project is going well?"

"Had to double-shift through much of the night after losing my engineer, but we're on schedule." Edward suppressed a yawn. Sleep called, but lunch was more enticing. It wasn't the food that mattered; Charlotte had sent an invitation to join her. Sleep could wait. He pointed at the wrecked body. "I was hoping you could tell me what happened." Whilst he related events in the launch bay, Edward studied the device Lister had removed from the skull. Unsettling as it was, the engineer in him was fascinated. "I didn't realize they could survive with so little brain tissue."

"Well, we need some space, but it's right-side only. It's mostly emotional and creative functions there, and we've found they actually work better without it. The left is mostly motor control and the like, so we preserve that."

"I see," he said, studying the body. Curiosity had got him now. "And-" he hesitated, wondering how to phrase his next question. Taking a lesson from Charlotte, he decided to be direct. "I must say I'm surprised. I'd heard they were neutered." He pointed at the groin.

"No, not anymore. We found it to be unnecessary, and as with animals, the procedure can cause many complications." Circling the table, Lister began explaining his craft.

His enthusiasm suggested his work usually got little attention. But it went beyond that, Edward thought. It was intentionally kept distanced from a society that wanted to look the other way. How many of the proponents of conversion had ever seen a place like this? He suspected the Earl of Warwick's wife might be rather less enthusiastic if she saw the business end of the process. She'd probably just be sick.

"So what happened to this one?" he asked, refocusing on their current problem. "Did it malfunction?"

"I don't know." Sighing, he moved to rub his head, but again, saw the blood and stopped. "I can't find a damn thing wrong with it. Or any of the others."

"You've had more?"

"Eleven failures in the last twenty four hours." He nodded. "That's not unusual in itself – we have hundreds, and they do burn out – but it's new ones that are failing, instead of the old. This one barely lasted a day!"

"You can't account for it?" Edward looked at the implants laid out on the table.

"No," he admitted. "Older ones do commit suicide occasionally. It's like they know they're breaking down. They'll sometimes jump overboard. I even saw one leap into a furnace, once. But there's no recorded incident of a marionette ever attacking a man. I can't believe it set out to kill your engineer."

"Why not?"

"They can't." Lister took a pair of forceps, and delved inside the skull. He extracted an implant that looked rather like a metal spider. "They all have a Kohlberg inhibitor. This bridges certain areas of the mind. It's their conscience, if you like. After surgery, they're docile anyway, but this makes sure."

"It couldn't have been tampered with? By creationists, perhaps?"

"The system is incredibly complex. It would take more than just a few misguided agitators to do it. And surely they'd be the last to have the skills, anyway."

"You may have been away too long," Edward replied. "They no longer confine their activities to demagoguery, and they are no longer just 'a few'. Their movement gathers pace all the time. A few months ago they plotted to bomb the natural history museum in London. Since they've failed to discredit Darwin's work, they now aim to destroy the evidence for it. All life-sentenced, of course," he added.

"Preposterous!"

"Agreed, but that makes them no less dangerous. More so, in fact: how can you reason with such people? Their 'new crusade' calls for the destruction of any ideas or technologies not mentioned in the Bible."

"They'd have us back in the dark ages?" Lister scoffed.

"Basically, yes." Edward looked at the body again. How much had the man known? Was he a foot soldier, or commander? He tried to apply logic to the problem. "We know there were at least two of them, and that they wanted to stop us from sailing. So they must remain prime suspect. Wait," he said, as another, even darker thought occurred. "These people hold their beliefs so strongly that no amount of evidence can sway them. Doctor-"

"Thomas."

"Thomas," he continued, "could those beliefs – those plans – be strong enough to survive the conversion process?"

"No. Impossible." He indicated the open skull. "Right brain, remember? Marionettes cannot 'believe' in anything."

"Very well." Another explanation lost. "Tell me this, then: how can you be so sure they weren't tampered with?"

"I'll show you." He led Edward back to the main lab. "This one is just completed." Thomas gestured at the girl.

"She's alive?"

"Of course." After tossing his stained gloves, he unlocked a cabinet full of small boxes. Taking one from the stack, he unpacked a glass cylinder similar to the one he'd just extracted from the Jack. It looked like a vacuum tube, but more complex. "This is the telmemric coupler – the critical component."

Edward watched him open a port in the scalp, and insert the device.

"The Aldini solution ends her trance state." He grabbed a syringe, and injected a dose into her neck.

The effect was instantaneous. Her eyes were open before the needle was out. As Thomas stepped back, she jerked upright, gasping for air.

"Incredible." Aware his eyes had settled on her chest, Edward looked away. He felt relief as his colleague put the girl into a gown. It wasn't only his own reaction that bothered him; it was the absence of hers. There was no emotion, not even confusion, let alone embarrassment. Without a sense of self, she was really was just a puppet. No more.

"All these components are factory fresh," he said, guiding her into a chair. "And aboard ship, only I have access. Tasking, as I'm sure you know, is primed by the ship's bells. The chimes switch them between functions." He tapped her head port.

"So what about the bells? Could someone be using them to-"

"The ampliphone suite is always under tight security. And anyway, they're just bells! The signal has no inherent meaning – it's just a switch, like I said." He opened a cabinet to reveal a device that looked like a small orchestrion. "This replicates the system, for training." He inserted a brass cylinder. "Only audible in here, of course. Don't want every Jack and Jill aboard to come running." He hit a switch. As the chimes sounded, the girl rose. Her vacant expression cleared, and she looked at Lister as if expecting orders. When he activated another chime, she remained standing, but went limp.

"So, we're still none the wiser," Edward sighed. Maybe there was nothing to find. Perhaps Maxwell's death had simply been what it appeared to be: a freak accident. It seemed a poor explanation to offer his wife.

"Damn it!" Lister started flicking switches on the console.

"What's wrong?"

"She's stopped responding," he groaned. "Not another one! We can't keep losing them at this rate." He tried again, but when the chimes sounded, the girl kept staring into space. After lighting his pipe, he began to pace back and forth. "Could be a faulty governor, I suppose." He shone a tiny flashlight into the girl's eyes.

"Have you consulted Lady Holden?" Edward asked. "Perhaps she could suggest something."

"I'd rather not. Not yet, anyway."

"Not willing to accept defeat, eh?" Edward smiled. "I'm the same."

"Yes. That, and the fact I've heard she's a-"

Snarling, the girl launched herself at Lister, clawing at his face. She pushed forward, keeping him off balance. Moving faster than Edward would have thought possible, she batted Lister's flailing arms aside, and clamped her hands around his throat.

"Get her off!" he gasped.

Edward grabbed her from behind, but she was far from an easy opponent. Her small body seemed to contain disproportionate strength. Taking hold of her wrists, he managed to pry her hands off Lister's neck.

He succeeded in wrestling her away, but the moment he relaxed, she broke free and escaped over the work bench. Even then, she wasn't done. Instead of running, she snatched up a broken Erlenmeyer flask and lashed out.

Edward withdrew his hand as the glass came down. The neck smashed on the bench, driving shards into her fist.

"Get ready!" Lister yelled, sprinting around the lab. Whilst the girl was distracted, he pounced, forcing her down onto the bench. "Take out the coupler. Now!"

Edward fumbled with the latch for a moment before opening the port, but managed to grasp the device. With a counter-clockwise twist, he yanked it out.

It was like flipping an off switch. Without so much as a moan, she collapsed, sliding down to rest on the floor.

"Are you alright?"

"Yes, thanks to you." Lister examined his neck in a mirror.

"What the hell just happened?"

"I– I don't know," he stuttered. "It was no faulty component, I'll tell you that. It was like she was completing a task. Keep taking plates until the table is clear. Keep peeling potatoes until they're all done. Attack until the target is dead." He turned white. "Come with me." He rushed through to the storage area. Like corpses, the new Jacks were stored on gurneys that retracted into cabinets.

"Is this wise?" Edward asked, as Lister pulled out another Jill.

"She can't break the straps." After inserting a coupler, he administered the injection.

Within ten seconds of activation, the girl began thrashing, trying to break free. Her urge to attack was sufficiently strong that she craned to snap at Lister's hand whilst he removed the coupler.

With shaking hands, Lister repeated the experiment on a Jack. It produced exactly the same result.

"Oh, God. Edward, this could be a system-wide failure. If they're somehow interpreting a new task as an order to attack…"

"We need to contact the Captain immediately," Edward said. "If the marionettes are malfunctioning, everyone is in danger."

"We'll have to start shutting them all down," Thomas agreed.

He reached for the televox handset, but with a clicking sound of electrical feedback, the campliphone cut in. A moment later, the ship's bells began to sound.

Counting eight chimes, Edward looked at his watch. Twelve PM. Lunch service was beginning. The waiting staff would be there. Dozens of them. Charlotte would be there.

He ran.

SIX

Edward dashed through the service corridors. Concealed deep within the ship, the area around the laboratory was deserted. It was fortunate, for in his haste, he had gone unarmed.

As he arrived at a staircase, he noticed a fire point nearby. He'd passed dozens of them every day without a thought. Now, it could be useful. He opened the door beside the hose, and took out the axe. It was a poor substitute for a gun, but would do.

He climbed up. The stairs delivered him onto the lower berth deck. Ahead, a Jill was emptying a laundry basket into a chute.

Be calm, he thought. She might be unaffected. Keeping to the opposite wall, Edward passed behind her with the axe ready.

She ignored him, and continued loading the chute.

After pausing at a guide map, he ran for the nearest elevator. Whilst the mechanism whirred away, he offered a quick prayer. With luck, there was still time.

Emerging onto the main deck, he began the long run down the central arcade. Here at least, things appeared normal. Passengers milled about in the shops. Most looked happy. Judging by the looks he got, his axe was the main source of concern.

Edward had just begun to consider that he'd overreacted when someone screamed.

"Get it off!" someone yelled.

Inside an ice-cream parlor, a Jill was grappling with a woman. Two men pulled her away, but misunderstanding the nature of the attack, released her.

She leapt forward, and swept up a heavy knife from the serving counter. Before they could react, she whirled around and rammed it into the throat of the man behind. She withdrew the blade to swipe at the next man, but he had just enough time to step away. That cleared her path.

Howling, she charged her original target.

Cowering in fear, the woman had no chance. The hand she extended in appeal was nearly severed as the girl slashed down. Again, she went for the throat, cutting deep into the flesh. Then she froze, perhaps confused by the blood spraying into her face.

Edward struck whilst she was distracted, landing a solid blow between her shoulder blades. As she fell, he lifted the axe and struck again. His aim was poor, but the impact broke her neck anyway. Looking at her smashed body, he expected to feel sick, but felt nothing. For now, some evolved instinct was in charge. Survival came first.

"Be quiet!" he shouted, as chatter broke out. "You must prepare to defend yourselves."

Shouting from further down the arcade signaled another incident. Gunfire came from somewhere forward. It was spreading. The dining room was still a long way. He left, yelling instructions to find the nearest marines.

A Jill lunged for him as he crossed a lounge, but he sidestepped the attack. One well-timed blow knocked her down. Two Jacks, their uniforms already torn, were advancing on a group of children. A terrified girl, no more than eight or nine herself, kept a little boy behind her, trying to shield him.

Edward swerved toward them without any conscious thought.

Surprise gifted him the first blow, but he hit the man's arm. He went down, crashing into an armchair, but was back up almost immediately.

Wary of the axe, the two men began to circle around the furniture, seeking an opportunity to attack.

Waiting was no use. If he allowed them to attack together, he was doomed. Edward glanced left and right. Which one first?

The first Jack leapt over the coffee table, taking the decision from him.

Edward dodged, parrying the blow with the axe handle, but when he turned back, the second man was already on him. He tried to strike, but more hands grabbed him from behind, dragging him back. I'm finished, he thought.

Gunfire flashed from his right. The Jack went down, bleeding from half a dozen wounds. Marines advanced across the lounge, exterminating the marionettes.

"Alright, sir?"

"Yes, yes. Thank you." Turning to address his rescuer, Edward found the soldier was little more than a child himself. The marine couldn't have been more than eighteen.

"Doctor Rankine?" It was the lieutenant he'd met on boarding. "Can you use this?" he asked, holding out a pistol.

"Of course," he replied. In truth, his skills were rusty. He hadn't fired a weapon since completing his national service. "How bad is it?" He ejected the clip, found it full, and replaced it.

"Bad. Marionettes are going crazy all over the ship. They're attacking on sight. We've been ordered to fall back and secure vital areas."

"But-" A sniffle from behind reminded him the children were still huddled in the corner. "What about the passengers?" he whispered.

"Ship first." He shook his head.

Anger flared before Edward realized they were right. He glanced out the windows. The headland to the south was covered in snow. The sea was now solid, a vast ice floe that yielded only due to the colossal power of the decay engines. Nothing could survive here. If the ship foundered, they were all doomed anyway.

"We need to go," the lieutenant said, organizing his men.

"Wait a minute." Edward tried to think. The lifeboats might do. They were elevated on launch rails, and it seemed unlikely the marionettes would start searching them. There would be supplies aboard, too. Trying to project confidence, he told the children to head for them and stay there. For now, it was the best he could do.

"Come on!" the lieutenant hissed.

Moving in formation, they reached the central concourse. A battle was being fought, and lost.

The floor was strewn with bodies. Some were puppets, but most were passengers. Equal opportunity killers, the marionettes had murdered men, women and children without preference. Here and there, survivors fought on, but there were fewer with each minute that passed. Swarming like locusts, the Jacks overran a group of men near the doors. When they moved off, only bodies remained. At the far end, a few marines were holding the balcony.

"Sir?" the young marine said. It was only a single word, but his intention was perfectly clear.

"No." The lieutenant patted an empty gun belt. "We don't have the ammunition."

The same problem accounted for the marines already amongst the bodies. On an exploration deployment, the crew was ill-equipped for war. They'd been carrying only a few rounds.

"Come on," he said, through gritted teeth. "We'll have to go around." He led them out onto the verandah before they were seen.

"Wait." Edward stopped. "I need to reach the dining room."

"No, you need to come with us. The Captain may need you."

"I have to go."

"Are you crazy?" a marine gasped. "It'll be full of them!"

"That's why I'm going. How I can I get there?"

Something in his tone must have registered, for the argument he'd expected from the lieutenant never came. He simply nodded.

"The breezeways run over the spar deck roof. It'll likely be deserted." He pointed at a ladder. "Hatch forty-nine will bring you in close to the dining room. That's your best chance."

SEVEN

If he'd stopped to think, Edward would have realized that attempting the journey over the top of the ship without winter clothing was stupid. Used only for observation and maintenance, the breezeway was open on both sides. A blast furnace in reverse, the Arctic-chilled wind stripped the life from him as he walked.

By the time he reached hatch forty-nine, he was on the cusp of serious frostbite. The only consolation was the pain. He knew that as long as it continued, his flesh still lived. Struggling to control his hands, Edward climbed inside and cranked the hatch shut.

He hunkered down, shaking. His hands tingled as if held too close to a roaring fire. A worrying shade of purple had spread down his fingers – and other extremities, he imagined – but after a few minutes the color began to fade.

When his hands obeyed his commands once more, he recovered the pistol from his pocket and set off down the narrow service corridor. Thankfully, no one was here; he was in no condition for a fight. A steep staircase discharged him back into the opulence of the public areas. He struggled to keep his bearings, and took several wrong turns before realizing he needed to be on the deck below.

Keeping his pistol ready, he descended the main staircase. A Jill lay on the landing, but was no threat. She'd been shot. Two more were down outside the dining room. Many passengers lay with them, but Edward allowed himself to entertain a little hope. It looked like they'd put up a fight, at least.

He went inside.

The dining room looked like an abattoir. The people in the first sitting for lunch had been butchered as comprehensively as the roasted meat on the tables. Bodies lay slumped over chairs. Others were on the floor. A group just inside the starboard doors had obviously been massacred whilst running for escape. They'd been stabbed in the back. Others had similar wounds, but most seemed to have been killed with bare hands.

Edward tried to focus on the faces, and began to recognize a few. The rotund woman he'd helped Rupert escort out had been strangled. A slim figure lying in a pool of blood turned out to be the Earl of Warwick's wife. Of him, there was no sign.

He found no sign of Charlotte, either. It was of course possible that she'd escaped. She may never even have arrived. Her lunch invitation had meant a great deal to him, but he was not so foolish as to think it held equal value to her. She could also be lying dead elsewhere. Standing amongst the human wreckage, Edward considered leaving. It might be better not to know. Better not to see her like that.

He went through to the buffet area anyway.

Even having seen the carnage in the dining room, it was shocking. The fighting in here had been brutal. Passengers and crew had died, but had taken a lot of marionettes with them. A Jill sat upright against the wall. She was dead, but a carving fork had been rammed through her neck, pinning her to the woodwork. Several Jacks bore deep slash wounds, which presumably accounted for the blood sprayed across the serving counters.

Hearing footsteps, Edward whirled around, lifting the pistol. It took him several seconds to realize the blood-soaked creature approaching was Charlotte. She carried a pair of huge knives. A second after that, he realized she was attacking. She thought he was one of them.

"It's me!"

She stopped, but kept a knife between them.

"Charlie, it's me. Oh God," he whispered, looking at the blood. "How badly are you hurt?"

"Edward," she panted. "What are you doing here?" She looked at the blood coating her arm, and finally seemed to grasp his concern. "Oh." She lowered the knife. "It's not mine."

"You're alright?"

"I managed to get a gun from a dead marine," she whispered. Her eyes glazed over. Just as he was sure she was about to break down, she seemed to shake it off. "After that, I used these." She hefted the knives. "Edward, what's going on?"

"I don't know." Keeping it short, he explained what little he could. "Are you alone?"

"No. There are a few others back there." She nodded toward the kitchen.

"Alright," he said, thinking. They couldn't stay here. "Get them together. We have to get to the bridge."

"But-"

"It's alright. I know a way." He looked at her dress. It was fashioned for style, not warmth. "But it's outside. We'll need more clothes."

"Well," she said, looking around at the bodies, "there's no shortage of those."

EIGHT

"Okay – four guns," Charlotte said. She passed his pistol back. "Five rounds for each."

"That's it?" Edward completed the depressing arithmetic in silence; the number was too pathetic to speak aloud. He wormed forward to look over the edge of the wheelhouse roof. The journey here had been easy, but entry looked impossible.

Below, the bridge was surrounded. Dozens of marionettes pounded on the screens. The red smudges decorating the structure said their hands would break long before the armored glass, but whilst they couldn't get in, neither could anyone else. Going down there with so little ammunition would be suicide.

"We need to think of something," she said, pulling her dinner jacket tight. "Quickly." By taking clothes from progressively overweight corpses, they'd managed to build up enough layers to afford some protection, but it had limits. "They can't stay out much longer, especially the children."

"Agreed." Edward looked at the rag-tag group behind them before rubbing at his eyes. Reflection from the ice seemed to be causing something akin to snow blindness. Mild at first, the pain had escalated into a terrible burning sensation. He was struggling to see, much less think.

"Over here!" Behind them, two men pulled at a roof hatch, but the heavyweight steel lid was sealed tight. In desperation, another man swung an axe at the hinge.

"Stop!" Edward hissed, pointing over the edge. "They'll hear!" But so would the crew, he realized. The trick was to tell them it wasn't yet more puppets on the roof.

He knelt beside the hatch, and began tapping with the butt of his pistol. No reply came. Was his Morse so poor as to be unrecognizable? Trying to recall the sequence, he rapped another message on the cold steel.

"Get back," the man snapped, lifting the axe again.

"Wait!" A succession of taps came from inside. His interpretation was poor, but best-guessing, he sent a reply. Surely any coherent message confirmed that a human had sent it?

It seemed his logic was flawed. No return message came. Edward was close to despair when the hatch popped open.

"Thank G-" A gun barrel appeared from inside, extinguishing his relief. "We're human!" he gasped. What else was there to say?

"Get in here. Quick."

No further encouragement was required. Fearing assault from both the enemy and the environment, they hustled inside.

"Bring blankets!" Captain Fitzjames ordered. "And rum – Ensign, there's a bottle in my fly quarters. Fetch it." He turned back. "Miss Redpath. Are you alright?"

"Yes, Captain." Shivering, she nodded at the children. "But they need attention."

"Indeed. Always take care of your soldiers, eh?" Turning away, he addressed the group with a degree of child-friendliness that took Edward by surprise. Rather than fearing him, the youngsters seemed reassured by the mechanically-augmented officer. "Some crewmen aren't much older when they enter the service," he said, obviously noting Edward's reaction. "You!" The captain pointed at a midshipman. "Get Beattie to look them over. He's acting surgeon."

"Sir." The man gathered the children, and led them away.

"Lister didn't make it here?" Edward enquired.

"Lister didn't make it at all." The moment the children moved on, Fitzjames' mask slipped. He looked tired. "Killed trying to reach the ampliphone suite, apparently."

"Blast." *Another good man dead. And the one most likely to pull us out of the fire.* "What is the situation, sir?"

"Well, as the saying goes, there's good news and bad." He crossed to the wall, and began tapping points on the huge illuminated ship plan. "The good news is that by falling back, we've managed to secure the critical areas. In addition to the bridge, engineering is locked down, as are the turrets. We also hold the ampliphone suite, for what it's worth," he added, sounding bitter.

"I assume the marionettes aren't responding to the bells?" It seemed Lister had died for nothing, if that had been his plan.

"You assume correctly."

"And the bad news?" Charlotte asked, joining them.

"We hold nothing else. Those bastards have free run of the *Dominator*." He nodded at her. "Please excuse me."

"I've heard far worse," she assured him. "Alright, then. How do you propose we retake her?"

"We don't." If Fitzjames felt any affront at a woman taking the initiative, he didn't show it. "We have neither the men nor the ammunition. But, as long as we hold these areas, we still control the ship. We've broadcast the emergency action signal. The *Destrier* has already sailed from Halifax with a commando battalion. We shall reverse course, rendezvous, and eliminate the problem."

"I see." She frowned. "But is there nothing we can do for the passengers?"

"Unless you propose close-quarters combat with nigh-on a thousand puppets, they'll have to fend for themselves for now. The ship is vast. Hopefully a good number of them have found somewhere to hide." His tone didn't match the words; for all his pragmatism, he obviously hated leaving them to their fate.

"How long before we can expect to reach the *Destrier*?" Edward asked, looking out over the forecastle. The marionettes continued to beat against the screens. All sound was muted by the thick glass, but their energy appeared undiminished. They wanted in.

"Once we've come about, we'll reach them in twenty-four hours at flank speed."

"Right." Edward watched the scenery passing behind the bows. It seemed agonizingly slow, but there was a limit to how fast a quarter mile-long ship was going to turn. The white glare set off his eyes again. Tears began streaming down his cheeks before he could wipe them away.

"Ice blindness," Fitzjames said. "You stayed outside too long."

"That would seem to be my fault," Charlotte said. "Doctor Rankine journeyed forward over the roof to come and find me."

Fitzjames looked at him. He said nothing, but Edward got the feeling his stock had just gone up a little.

"Hold on." After rummaging around in a drawer, he passed Edward a small glass phial.

"What is it?"

"Cocaine. Rub it into your eyes. Old explorer's trick."

He looked at the bottle. It seemed insane, but after his night in the Crow's club, what difference did it make? It was a bit late to worry about drugs now. It felt strange, but worked wonderfully.

"Better?" Charlotte asked.

"Hmn. Completely numb already."

"Really? I might try it," she murmured. She tried to wipe the blood from her neck, but it had dried on. Charlotte declined the phial when he offered it, but accepted rum from one of the crew. Abandoning any pretense of etiquette, she ignored the glass and tipped back the bottle before passing it to him.

Sheltered, and anaesthetized by the cocktail of tropane and alcohol, Edward finally stopped shivering. Within a few minutes his temperature came up, and he took off his overcoat. Another drink made him feel better still.

"Edward, what could do this to them?" Charlotte asked, removing an oversized shirt.

"I don't know. Even Lister couldn't understand it." Looking like a pair of life-size Babushka dolls, they continued shedding layers until comfortable. He recounted what he'd learned during his visit to the laboratory. "All of which begs the question, why did he go for the ampliphone suite?" Through the rum haze, he considered the captain's news. "If he didn't believe that could be the cause, why risk his life trying to reach it?

Edward passed the rum back, and looked outside again. The marionettes were still there, trying to break through with hands that had been reduced to bloody messes. It seemed none of them had thought of using tools to breach the glass. Hopefully, it would stay that way. He had the feeling that the explanation for all this should be obvious, that the pieces were all visible, yet the answer eluded him. Wishing he hadn't partaken of the rum, he tried to focus, but was denied the chance.

A klaxon wailed, breaking the already weak links in his mind.

"Now what?" Fitzjames appeared behind them. "Report!"

"Someone's activated the fire system," a seaman called.

Inwardly, Edward fought despair. It seemed some higher power was conspiring to finish them. A fire would kill them just as surely as their attackers. They couldn't possibly abandon ship here.

"Where?"

"Lever four-nine-two was pulled." He consulted a wall chart. "That's compartment sixteen, abaft turret five, sir."

Edward joined him, casting his eye over the vast array of gauges. Several of the needles were flicking back and forth. "What is this?"

"Uh – temperatures, sir, for each section."

He stared at the dials. Although still erratic, the needles were definitely climbing.

"We have a fire, sir," the seaman said, his tone rising in time with the needles.

"Cut in the extinguishers."

"Extinguisher pumps, aye." He pulled a set of levers.

Tumblers set beside them began spinning. The gallon indicators were a blur, but the temperature gauges continued to climb. One shot into the red zone.

"This one is the launching bay, isn't it?" Edward asked, tapping the dial.

"Yes, sir, it is." Frowning, the seaman checked his chart. "How do you know the numbers?"

"I don't." He turned back to Fitzjames. "This isn't a fire – at least, not a normal one."

"How can you be so sure?"

"Only one thing could generate that much heat so fast." Behind him, a warning bell sounded. "Some of the capacitrons have been activated."

NINE

Two marines hurried to the next junction, and covered the corridors whilst the group passed through. As they picked up the rear, another pair advanced to take point. The cyclic formation ensured the center of the group was never exposed. And there walked Edward, suddenly the most valuable person on the ship.

He'd tried to replicate the marines' technique – constant movement, weapon always ready – but had given up after a few minutes. It didn't make him feel any safer, and the weight of his mini-maxim made it tiring. The impressive device combined a compact machinegun with a sawn-off shotgun for boarding actions, but Edward doubted he would hit anything. Not intentionally, anyway.

Relegated to the role of a fragile cargo, he busied himself trying to prepare for his task. It was no longer possible to believe these events were coincidence. The activation of the capacitrons was no more an accident than the marionette attacks. Someone, probably those damn fool creationists, meant to sabotage the expedition, even if it meant sinking the ship.

So long as the extinguishers kept dowsing the devices, they might stay cool enough to be safely launched. If they didn't – well, there seemed to be little value in thinking about it. Even the lifeboats they'd launched with a few of the women and children aboard would be destroyed. They lacked the speed to reach a safe distance, although he still wished Charlotte had taken the chance to try. Instead, she was here, heading straight into danger. He glanced at her. Despite the tight smile he got in reply, he wished she was somewhere else. Anywhere else. Preoccupied, Edward almost barged into the men in front when they slowed.

"Hold!" a Marine hissed.

Ahead, the men changed formation, sweeping the stairwell. They fired at someone he couldn't see, their suppressed weapons emitting a sharp tapping sound. A Jill tumbled down to land at their feet. *The baffling in the moderators is breaking down.* Silence was safety, but after several such encounters, the weapons were now worryingly loud.

They stepped over the body and moved on, but the damage was done. A piercing shriek suggested that they'd been heard, and moments later, feet began thumping on the polished floor. Jills, all in waitress attire, burst in from the promenade deck. One broke a window in her haste. Blood sprayed from an arterial cut, but she paid the wound no heed, and charged with her sisters.

Short on time, the marines raked the group with automatic fire. Their attackers were eliminated, but valuable ammunition was spent. Worse still, the gas pressure finished off the suppressors; the weapons were now almost back at normal volume.

A long howl echoed down the corridor, then another. Enraged wails overlapped in an obscene parody of harmonized singing.

"Go!" the lieutenant yelled, abandoning stealth.

Marionettes flooded the section as they ran, pouring in from all sides. Men holding the flanks fell almost immediately. Unable to reform amongst the melee, the phalanx disintegrated.

Edward lifted his gun as a Jack charged. He fired, but discharged a shotgun cartridge by mistake. It did the job. At close range, the shot struck as a single mass, causing tremendous damage.

"There's too many!" the lieutenant gasped, firing. "With me!"

He led them into another corridor. Funneled toward the guns by the narrow space, the puppets made easy targets, but there were simply too many. For each one that fell, two more stepped forward, eager to take their place.

"This can't work!" Edward selected single shot, and shot a Jack trying to crawl beneath his fallen comrades. He required no military training to process the situation. It was simple mathematics. Their ammunition was running out.

Then it became even worse. Behind him, Charlotte fired at a group advancing from the arcade. They were surrounded. Half her rounds went into the ceiling as the muzzle climbed, but others joined in. The fusillade broke the charge.

"Right – you two go for the elevator!" The lieutenant used the respite to push a fresh magazine home. "Mills, Hudson, go with them." He picked off a Jill as she burst from a storeroom. "The rest of us will lead them off."

"But-"

"Go! We have to buy time to get you away."

"Alright." Edward caught his eye, and immediately regretted it. The man's choice of words was entirely too accurate. Time could be bought, but the currency would be their lives. He felt compelled to say something, but what? Nothing would make any difference.

"Just get it done," the lieutenant snapped. After ordering the remaining men to form two groups, he gave them a final nod. "Now!"

The marines charged.

Edward waited for Mills to lead off before pushing Charlotte after him. Then he followed, with Hudson bringing up the rear. They didn't get far.

As Mills slowed to check a blind corner, a huge Jack tackled him like a rugby player. His momentum sent them crashing into the wall. Edward moved in, firing into the man's ribs almost point blank as they slid to the ground. The shot was lethal, but Mills' neck was already broken.

"Leave him!" Charlotte shouted, as Hudson knelt beside the body. "He's gone!"

Hudson rose as another attack came. Wielding shovels like battleaxes, a group of oil-covered engineering Jacks hurled themselves forward.

Three guns working in concert proved sufficient to repel the attack. Turning to cover Charlotte, Hudson shot a Jill trying to slash at her with a knife. Edward killed a Jack advancing whilst the marine's back was turned.

When Charlotte aimed to repay the favor, her gun clicked empty. Expecting support, Hudson was late in bringing his weapon to bear. A Jack ended his fight with a colossal blow to the head. Striking side-on, the shovel cleaved flesh from bone. Hudson collapsed, screaming as his face peeled away from his skull.

Edward fired his second shotgun cartridge.

After checking they had time, Charlotte did likewise, but she aimed down. Her shot ended Hudson's agony.

"Come on!" he yelled, dragging her away. Sorrow would have to wait, assuming they survived.

A short dash took them to the service elevator. After slamming the gate shut, Edward hit the button for engineering. Nothing happened. Swearing, he punched the button again.

Their pursuers arrived as the elevator began to descend. Arms snaked between the bars, grasping for them, but they dropped out of reach. Concerned that trapped limbs might overload the mechanism, Edward drove them back with his remaining rounds.

Above them, one Jill waited too long before withdrawing her arm. Accompanied by tortured howls, her limb was ripped free at the shoulder.

Edward dropped his empty gun, and drew the Webley revolver the captain had given him. It was a poor substitute, but it was all they had. Or so he thought.

"Turn around for a second," Charlotte said, tossing her own weapon. "Go on!"

When he turned back, she was holding a compact pistol. Looking at the outfit she wore, he couldn't fathom where she'd concealed it. He opened his mouth.

"A gentleman wouldn't ask," she said, working the slide.

The elevator continued down.

TEN

The watertight doors leading to the launch bay had been cranked shut. After twirling the release, Edward eased the door open with the intention of sneaking a look, but was forced back by a blast of steam.

When it dissipated, he ventured inside. Visibility was down to just a few yards. He kept his pistol up, but nothing emerged from the steam to challenge them. The bay had been transformed into a giant sauna. Water spraying from the overhead extinguishers was running down toward the stern doors, where it pooled in the trough beneath the discharge racks. The vast plume of steam billowing from the water confirmed his worst fears. It was impossible to see through the superheated vapor, but the capacitrons in launch position were obviously active.

"Where's the door control?" Charlotte asked. The previously dry blood was running off her; the volume of steam had soaked them in seconds.

"It's not that simple." Edward tried to think. Thankfully, the active devices were already in launching position. But when the doors opened, the water would be the first thing out. "I have to check them first. They could overload if we drain the bay. Come on."

He led her to the control station. With Charlotte watching his back, he tried to establish temperatures. The instruments were dead, probably unable to function in the intense humidity.

"Alright, then," he said, wiping sweat from his eyes. "We'll have to chance it." Whilst struggling into an asbestos fire suit, he explained his plan. "Wait for me to release the clamps. Once the capacitrons are free, we'll open the doors. The water should take them out." He gestured at his head. "I need a hand."

"Be careful." After checking the suit was secure, she helped him into his gloves, like a mother putting mittens on a toddler. She gave him a smile before lifting the hood into place.

Edward started toward the doors. Sealed inside the suit, he began to sweat even faster. As he climbed the ladder to the walkway above the discharge racks, the temperature soared. This close to the active decay cores, the heat was incredible. Without protection, he would have been burned terribly. Even with the suit, he knew he didn't have long.

He collected a wrench, and began to release the clamps. The heavy gloves robbed him of dexterity, but after a few minutes, all four active devices were loose in the water, bobbing about like potatoes boiling on the stove. Edward retreated to a safe distance before removing the hood.

"Charlotte!" he called, shrugging off the suit. "Get ready-"

Something struck him with incredible force. He tried to recover, but smashed into a bench. He went down, tools clattering to the floor with him. Dazed, he tried to focus through the pain. When he looked up, Samuel was standing over him.

The giant lifted an arm.

"No, wait," he gasped. "Your orders-"

Samuel ignored him, and lunged forward, but Edward managed to swerve the blow. The enormous fist landed on solid metal, but it appeared to cause him no discomfort.

Edward reached for his revolver, but the marionette grabbed his arm. Sweeping a hand across the floor, he found a hammer. He struck down. The drop-forged steel hit Samuel's foot, surely breaking bones. Seizing the chance, he scrambled upright and drew his revolver.

His first shot was a good hit to the chest. It produced no apparent effect. A second delivered the same lack of result. Samuel looked down, frowned, and then continued forward. His conversion must have included armor of some sort. Edward aimed high.

Samuel recoiled as the four-five-five Imperial round struck his forehead. Blood fountained from the wound, but the marionette steadied himself. The impact had torn a strip of flesh from his head, but metal lay beneath, not bone. His skull had been modified.

Gunfire came from above, and Samuel rocked again. Charlotte appeared opposite the pool, firing.

"No!" Edward yelled, as she started across the walkway. "Back!"

Moving whilst the creature was still distracted, Edward dashed around the flooded section and climbed up a ladder. He found Charlotte amongst the lifting machinery.

"It's pointless." Edward wiped sweat from his face. It was like trying to fight in a Turkish bath. "God knows what she's had done to him."

His remark seemed to tempt fate. Samuel appeared beneath them, visible through the grate floor. He'd obviously lost them in the steam. After searching around, he stopped. Taking hold of his jacket cuff, he ripped the right sleeve off. A metal section had been grafted into his forearm, with hoses running back under his armpit. A ventilated barrel hinged out, terminating at his wrist. He produced a pan magazine from his pocket, and attached it near his elbow. The man was a walking gun.

Samuel completed his circuit of the lower level. After another look around, his eyes turned upward. He lifted his arm, extending his thumb to act like a gun sight.

They ran. A shrill whine came from behind as rounds punched through the grating. Weaving between machinery, they tried to stay out of sight.

"We need more firepower." Now grateful for the steam, Edward checked around the corner before pulling Charlotte with him.

"Rupert has an elephant gun in his quarters," she supplied. "It's seven-hundred nitro express."

"Does he?" Edward snapped. Insanely, some part of his mind – the male part, no doubt – was still able to inject a surge of jealousy. *How does she know that?*

"Well, you come up with something!"

Another burst of gunfire tore through the grating. Rounds passed dangerously close before smacking into the bulkhead. Edward guessed he was firing blind, but that wouldn't make the bullets any less injurious if they hit. They changed direction, but then heard footsteps tapping on the metal stairs. Samuel was coming.

Halfway up, Edward saw him pause to reload. Samuel detached the empty magazine and replaced it with another. When he set off, he was moving noticeably slower.

When they sought cover behind the pumping equipment, he gave chase. After firing another burst, he was slower still. He staggered on, looking almost drunk.

"Of course!" Despite the situation, Edward smiled. He did have firepower, just of a very different type. "Ingenious!"

"What?" Charlotte asked, ducking behind the machinery.

"The weapon has no water jacket. His blood must act as the coolant."

"Nice." She grimaced. "How does that help us?"

"It's a clever idea, but flawed. His body can't possibly exchange enough heat, so his temperature is rising. Sustained fire will make him overheat."

"Are you sure?"

"Of course. Why?" The answer came to him just too late to stop her.

Charlotte bolted across the bay, diving behind the rack at the far end.

Samuel turned, sending a hail of fire after her. Rounds ricocheted off the walkway.

Taking a more circumspect approach, Edward picked up a pair of pliers and hurled them toward the control room.

Taking the bait, he swung and emptied the weapon. Pouring with sweat, Samuel began to reload, but fumbled the process. He seemed unable to locate the magazine on the port.

Edward looked over the edge. The capacitrons were directly below. He'd never get a better chance. He grabbed a wrench from the rack behind, and charged.

"No!" Lady Holden appeared in the control room. She climbed down, keeping a long-barreled target pistol trained on Edward. "Leave him!"

Charlotte appeared from the steam and piled into her. A gunshot went wide. Holden tried to claw her face, but Charlotte countered in an equally unladylike fashion. Sidestepping the attack, she landed a kick to her shin. When Lady Holden folded, Charlotte bought a knee up into her face.

Looking at his mistress, Samuel shouted something, or tried to, but the words came out as gibberish.

Edward struck. His blow caught Samuel under the chin, snapping his head back. He staggered back toward the edge. A second blow sent him over.

Arms flailing, the marionette toppled into the boiling water. He tried to pull himself out, but was unable to find purchase.

"Now!" Edward yelled.

Charlotte yanked the door release lever. A crack of daylight penetrated the murk as the hydraulics swung the heavy doors open. The lower bay drained, taking the active devices out to sea. Samuel went with them, floating face-down over the edge. They'd done it. The realization seemed to hit a biological off-switch. Overwhelmed by his exertions, he collapsed to his knees.

"Edward!" Charlotte screamed.

Her obvious terror sparked some Darwinian response; despite his exhaustion, fresh energy became available. Edward got to his feet. Marionettes were closing in, all armed with knives, axes or tools. He pulled Charlotte toward the walkway, but yet more appeared on the other side. They were surrounded. He looked out through the doors. An icy wake churned behind the stern. It might be a better fate.

"Stop!" Lady Holden wobbled to her feet. "No," she shouted, wiping blood from her nose. "Snare!"

The Jacks continued their advance, but lowered their weapons.

Edward tried to shove past them, but there were simply too many. He was restrained, wrestled back into place. Other puppets held Charlotte beside him.

Lady Holden waited until they were immobilized before approaching.

"You," she said, jabbing a finger at Edward, "just don't know when to die, do you?" She walked on before he could respond. After making sure the Jacks on either side of Charlotte had a tight grip, Holden stepped back, adjusted her position, then slapped Charlotte across the face.

Her face betrayed the pain for an instant. Then she replaced it with a smile, tainted by a freshly split lip. "You hit like a girl."

Holden stepped away, shaking with rage. At that moment, Edward fully expected to die, but instead of ordering their execution, she seemed to calm herself. "No. No," she repeated. "There'll be no quick ending for you. We shall find something slower." She smiled. "Bring!"

ELEVEN

The ballroom was busy, but there was no party atmosphere. Knife-wielding Jacks were keeping a group of survivors corralled near the bar. They looked terrified, but mostly intact.

"Hardly any wounded," Charlotte whispered, as they were shoved into the crowd.

"They weren't taking prisoners until she re-tasked them." After being held in isolation for several hours, it was a relief to see people alive, but the crowd was small. There were perhaps five hundred souls. Unless others were holding out elsewhere, thousands had been slaughtered. There were also very few children. Hopefully the bulk of those not already on the lifeboats were hidden away, hard to find. Edward decided to leave that line of thought there.

"Welcome to the party!" The Earl of Warwick was behind the bar, serving drinks. His demeanor suggested he'd also consumed a great many.

"Scotch?" Looking remarkably cheerful, Rupert popped up from under the counter with a bottle in each hand.

"I'll take one," Charlotte sighed.

Edward looked at the Jacks, but their only interest seemed to be watching for would-be escapees. "Might as well."

"Let's see. Ten years – twenty-five years oak-aged," he said, examining both labels. "Only the best for a beautiful lady." Winking, he filled her glass.

Charming to the end. And it could well be that. Jealousy seemed ridiculous. It was good to see him.

"And you, my friend." Rupert slid him another glass before gesturing around the corner. "Someone wants to see you."

Pushing through the crowd, they found Fitzjames sitting at the bar. He wasn't drinking.

"I assume our continued existence means your mission was a success?"

"Yes, for what good it did." With the bridge lost, there seemed to be no hope left. "Captain, we know-"

"Lady Holden," he finished. "She forced us to surrender control a short while ago. She started executing passengers." He shook his head. "Did it herself, too; no delegating it to the foot-soldiers. I gave in when she threatened to start on the children. The admiralty will no doubt disagree."

Edward looked at Charlotte. Since they could offer nothing that would ease his obvious torment, they related events in the loading bay. After all possible stories had been exchanged, conversation turned to the inevitable.

"What I still don't understand is why." Charlotte sipped her drink.

"For now, it doesn't matter. What matters is how." Fitzjames thumped the bar. "If we can establish her means of control, we might yet retake the ship." He looked at Edward. "Well?"

"Sir, I still don't know." Edward set down his drink. Tempting as it was, the liquor was unlikely to boost his brain function.

"What about that controller she used at dinner?" Charlotte asked.

"That couldn't possibly broadcast to the whole ship. Logic tells us she must have found a way of overriding their standard instructions, but I can't imagine how."

"In that case," she snapped, looking over his shoulder, "I suggest we just ask her."

All conversation died as Lady Holden entered the room, surrounded by a dozen armed Jacks. A few Jills completed the entourage.

Fearing a fresh assault, the passengers cowered back as she approached. No one wanted to make a target of themselves.

"If all of us attacked now, we might overwhelm them," Rupert whispered.

Fitzjames looked around the room before replying. "No. We keep the powder dry. For now." He got up. "Lady Holden."

"Captain." She stepped closer, but kept several of the largest Jacks between them.

"In accordance with Imperial maritime law, I hereby acknowledge your capture of HMS *Dominator*, and formally request your terms."

"My terms?" A smile crossed her face. There was nothing pleasant about it. "I have no terms."

"Then what is your purpose here?"

"Yes," Charlotte snapped, pushing forward to join Fitzjames. "At least tell us that. Why did all these people have to die?"

"They were simply in my way. Unfortunate, but there it is."

"Unfortunate?" Charlotte choked. "You're fu-"

"How dare you judge me!" she shouted. "You, of all people, are in no position to judge. This is your fault."

"What?" She shook her head. "Natalie, I truly have no idea how I've wronged you, but if this is between us, then keep it that way. Let the others go."

"Your ego knows no bounds, does it? It's not about you, you little brat. I don't waste my time on personal matters. It's business, no more."

"But – I don't understand," she stuttered. "You have no rival interests here. What could possibly-"

"You have no vision at all." Holden shook her head. "You're welcome to your piffling deals with the savages." She sighed. "Do you seriously imagine that I arranged access to Persia for oil, of all things? Once complete, my Trans-Imperial magneto-rail will render shipping redundant. The Gulf States were the last section of the route."

"This is all about money?" Edward gasped.

"Despite your intelligence, I see you have no vision, either. Trade is more than money, Doctor. Trade is power, influence. So long as the Northwest Passage remains closed, I will control all trade from the East." Excitement crept into her voice. "As a fringe benefit, we also gain a vast supply of subjects. We've converted millions already."

"But you can't possibly sell that many," Edward said, seeking solace in economics. It was preferable to contemplating the scale of her evil. Now, Rupert's news regarding her Persian operation made terrible sense. The locals hadn't been killed. They'd been marionised. "The market is too small."

"But they won't be sold, will they?" Fitzjames said. "They're not servants. They're soldiers."

"Ah, Captain!" she exclaimed, looking genuinely pleased. "I suppose I should have expected a military mind to grasp it. Yes, soldiers – my soldiers. Dear Samuel may be gone, but his legacy will live on. New models can be tasked with battle. With wealth, influence, and an army at my disposal, I shall control the Empire. I will make it great again. No more weakness, no more childish indulgences. Imagine what we shall achieve! We could conquer nature itself. We could reach the moon. Running on electricity, my trains will cross the Empire in mere hours. There will be no stopping us!"

"Electricity?" the Earl of Warwick whispered. "She's hysterical."

In one smooth motion, Lady Holden stepped forward, drew her pistol, and shot him.

"Help me!" Edward grunted, trying to arrest his fall. With others lending support, he lowered the Earl to the ground. Blood was spreading down his shirt, but only a little. In engineering terms, a simple explanation presented itself: there was no pressure. Sure enough, he found no pulse. The shot to the heart had killed him almost instantly.

"Was that really necessary?" he asked, when the screaming had stopped. Although aware it was foolish, he was unable to stop himself.

"Yet more blood on your hands, Doctor."

"Mine?"

"Yours. If you'd had the decency to get knifed in Badash, none of this would have been necessary. Even when your engineer died in your place, I still tried to limit the damage. I re-tasked the puppets once the capacitrons were armed. They would've allowed you to abandon ship. If you'd co-operated, we could all have simply sailed away, knowing that those lunatic creationists were responsible.

I'm not a monster." She frowned. "You bought this upon yourselves. You've left me no way to save you."

Edward abandoned the conversation. She was either insane, or entirely dispossessed of conscience. The end result was the same either way.

"If what you claim is true, then at least put any remaining children in lifeboats, those too young to understand," Fitzjames tried. "They can't possibly implicate you."

"In principle I would agree, but I'm afraid it would be pointless, Captain." She shrugged. "The lifeboats would never escape in time."

"In time for what?" Even as Edward asked, the answer arrived in his mind. Only one thing made sense.

"My soldiers have destroyed the turbo-pumps for the cooling system. According to the bridge instrumentation, the decay engines will soon overload. Regrettably, the *Dominator* will join that long list of ships the Navy has stupidly lost in the Arctic."

"You must not do this!" protested a well-spoken lady in the crowd. "You-"

Holden turned the pistol on her.

She closed her mouth.

"You have time to make your peace. Provided you don't try to escape, the marionettes will leave you alone. Spend it in prayer if you wish, but since you're all to die anyway, I recommend you try to enjoy yourselves." She looked around the room. "I see men are very much in the majority here. That's awkward." She smiled. "Since Lady Redpath is responsible, I suggest she might entertain you all," she said, staring at Charlotte. "It's the least she can do." With a final nod to the subject of her revenge, she backed toward the doors.

Acting on some shared common sense, no one spoke for at least a minute after she left. Then the whispering began. When the Jacks failed to respond, conversation followed, which rapidly escalated into argument.

Edward looked at the crowd. Some looked beaten, ready to lie down and die. Others looked ready to fight on. But others still, mostly those who'd raided the bar, were plainly thinking on Holden's words. If they were to die anyway, they might as well have fun. And Charlotte had been set up as their primary target.

"Now what?" he asked. The question was asked mainly from habit, and he had no expectation of an answer. It was just as well.

"Where's she going?" Charlotte frowned. "If the ship is going up in smoke, how does she get away?"

Everyone looked to Fitzjames.

"The *Dominator* has two interceptors in cradle docks. They're fast gunboats, designed to engage pirates and the like. She'll be taking one of those, I imagine. But that's a problem for later."

"We need to act fast," Rupert agreed, listening to the chatter. "It'll come apart now."

"Yes." Fitzjames stood. "Ladies and gentlemen-"

"We're done listening to you," a crewman shouted. "We're all dead anyway. Eh, lads? We-"

Fitzjames surged forward on his replacement legs, and grabbed the man by the throat. He slammed him against the wall before he could recover. A short struggle ensued whilst the man tried to break free. With a single rapid movement, the Captain twisted his neck. The struggling stopped.

"There will be no mutiny aboard this ship! We will have order." He looked around the room, challenging anyone to meet his stare. "Anyone else? No?" He released his grip. The limp body slid to the floor. "Then bear yourselves in a manner worthy of Her Majesty!"

Edward released the breath he'd been holding. He'd witnessed the start of a riot once, in London. This room now felt the same. It had been close, but it wasn't over yet.

Two men stood at the bar were drinking straight from the bottle. They looked around the room. Their gaze settled on a group of ladies seated nearby.

Moving away from the crowd, the Captain beckoned them to follow.

"Well done, sir," Rupert murmured.

"It won't last." He shook his head. "Death is little threat to these men now. I'm not sure they'll follow my orders. The ship's bells don't work on people, son."

Edward frowned, reflecting on his remark. Throughout the altercation in the bar, the Jacks had done nothing. He thought back to Lister's lecture. The marionettes' limitations meant tasks had to be loaded on a regular basis, yet Holden had done it without making a sound. He watched a Jack change position, blocking the path of a man trying to sidle toward the doors. Or had Holden simply issued orders without being heard? He wandered back toward the bar, still watching the marionettes.

"We're doomed!" a woman sobbed. "We're all going to die!"

"It's not over yet," Charlotte said. "Edward?" she whispered, following him. "What can we do?"

"We can think!" he replied, without taking his eyes from the Jacks.

The puppets continued their assigned tasks with the usual mechanical efficiency. Then one of the Jills patrolling the corridor stopped, her head cocked to one side. It was the manner of a dog. A dog responding to a call, Edward thought. When he looked around the room, he saw others behaving in the same fashion.

"Of course." With hindsight, it was obvious. "It's just sound, Charlie. She controls them with sound!"

"I can't hear anything," she objected.

"You don't have to – there are sounds both above and below the range of human ears. There are many things we don't hear."

"You mean like a dog whistle?"

"Precisely. Lister said the telmemric couplers were fresh from the factory. Those couplers must have been modified to respond to a signal – one that overrides the bell system and activates pre-loaded tasks."

"Like killing people."

"Right. So," he whispered, following his line of thought, "if we can find the source of that signal and disable it, their normal functions should cut back in."

"Go on."

"She'd need a sound generator, a device to send the signal." His mind completed the connections. "That's the key."

"The music box," Charlotte hissed. "But, Edward, it could be anywhere."

"Not so." He shook his head. "It would need a lot of energy to broadcast throughout the ship. She must have hacked into the ampliphone cabling, so it would have to be somewhere private, where no one would find it."

"Her stateroom?" she suggested.

"Yes – no. No. It might constitute evidence. She wouldn't risk that. But, since she'd planned for those supposed creationists to carry the blame, then…"

"Then she probably installed it in their stateroom," Charlotte finished.

Their eyes met.

"Edward." She smiled. "You're a genius."

"I hope you're right, because we still need a solution to our immediate problem: how the hell do we get out of here?"

"We're going to need a diversion of some kind," she agreed.

"Something like that." Edward studied their guards once more. An idea began to form. If his deductions were correct, there might be another possibility. If he was wrong, then he'd probably get himself killed, but it seemed there was little to lose. "Come on."

"Edward-" Charlotte began, watching a marionette step forward.

"Stay with me. Take it easy."

Taking great care to avoid any sudden movement, he walked over to the Captain. The marionettes watched closely, but held their position. Maybe it could work. Keeping his voice low, Edward shared his theory with Fitzjames.

"It sounds plausible enough," he said, rubbing his beard. "Alright. It has to be worth a try. The creationists – or whoever they were – were in cabin two-seventeen. We searched it after they were arrested." He looked at the few remaining marines before turning back to Edward. "Be right, Doctor. Without weapons, we'll take losses getting you out of here, but so be it. If we-"

"Sir, I think there's another option," he interrupted. "We might be able to confuse them enough for a few of us to slip away – and if not, at least gain an advantage."

"How?"

"Remember, marionettes are incapable of abstract thought. They only respond to external stimuli, so the order 'guard them' is meaningless to a Jack or Jill. They'll have been given specific instructions – 'keep them inside this room,' or 'kill anyone that goes for a weapon.' The trigger might even be vocal – if someone used the word 'attack' for example," he said, mouthing the critical word.

"I suppose," Fitzjames said, but he looked unconvinced.

"Think about it. It would be obvious to any human observer that we're plotting something, and yet they've done nothing! We haven't met any of the criteria to warrant action. So long as we avoid them, we're safe. We may be able to use that against them."

"But even if you're right, we don't know what the triggers are," Rupert pointed out. "That's a hell of gamble, Edward."

"Exactly what are you proposing?" Fitzjames asked.

"Lady Holden's signal activates their new tasks, but I don't believe it wiped out the old ones. So they should still be primed for whatever task they were completing when she activated the device." He looked at his watch.

"At least some of these were on lunch service," Charlotte said.

"That'll do." Edward took a deep breath. It was no use waiting. "Get ready," he warned, turning to face the nearest puppets. "Service! Lunch service, now!"

Nothing happened. Was his theory wrong? Then he noticed a Jill near the door hopping from foot to foot. Looking agitated, she set off toward the tables at the back of the room. A moment later, another followed, abandoning her post at the staircase. Two more followed, but there were still far too many watching them.

"Clearance!" Fitzjames yelled, staying perfectly still. "Clear the tables immediately!"

Another one left her post, heading toward the bar.

"Now or never," Charlotte murmured.

When Edward judged it couldn't get much better, they went for the door. Resisting the urge to run, they maintained a brisk walk to the corner.

"Edward, you did it!" she cried, checking behind them. "We're out!"

"Charlotte, we're aboard a ship full of killers, hundreds of miles away from help in the most inhospitable environment on Earth."

"Alright." She frowned. "You don't have to be so negative about it."

"Let's get out of here."

TWELVE

"It's that way," Charlotte insisted, pointing left. "I'm sure!"

Edward stuck his head around the corner to look in both directions, but the corridors were identical extensions of the featureless maze. Sighing, he retreated again. Their journey wasn't going to plan.

On the upside, they hadn't been attacked. On the few occasions they'd seen marionettes, it had been easy enough to dodge them. They'd also managed to arm themselves; the puppets' tasks obviously hadn't included collecting weapons from their victims. Fallen marines had furnished them with weapons and ammunition.

On the downside, they were lost.

"Alright," he conceded. Her sense of direction could scarcely be worse than his, and they were running out of time. If they delayed much longer, Holden would win by default. "Come on."

"There," she hissed, a few minutes later. Ahead, a ship's guide was displayed next to a noticeboard. "Told you." She tapped the plan. "That way."

Correctly orientated, they were finally able to decipher the complex numbering system used below decks. They worked their way deeper into the ship. A few minutes later, they closed in on their destination.

"Look." Edward indicated a cabin door. "Two hundred and thirty one – two hundred and thirty – we're almost there."

He led the way, silently counting down the numbers. They found their target cabin around the next corner. Edward couldn't read the door number, but he didn't need to.

A pair of Jacks stood outside, each holding an axe. It was in no way surprising, but that didn't make it any less unwelcome. It left them no quiet means of entry. Shooting the sentries would alert not only anyone inside, but any marionettes nearby.

"We'll have to move fast," Charlotte whispered, obviously reaching the same conclusion.

"Right." Edward was the kind of man who liked to plan everything in detail, but it simply wasn't an option. They were out of time. Sometimes, engineering was a matter of delicate adjustment. And sometimes, you just had to hit things with a sledgehammer. "On three?"

They mouthed the countdown together, and then darted around the corner.

Both Jacks fell easily. They scarcely managed to lift their axes before being cut down. Against all instinct,

Edward pressed on. Surprise was their only advantage; it could not be squandered through hesitation.

He barged through the door, but ran straight into the arms of another Jack. Edward tried to bring up his carbine, but the man grabbed the barrel, denying him the shot.

A shocking blast came from behind as Charlotte fired past him. It caused only a flesh wound, but the impact knocked his opponent back.

Edward fired before the Jack could recover. Delivered at short range, the bullet passed clean through his chest, and smashed a mirror behind. He fell, dead before he hit the floor.

He turned his gun toward a second man, but Charlotte beat him to it, rapid firing as the marionette charged.

The puppet's collapse revealed a third Jack, sitting at a desk. Edward turned his carbine toward the fresh target, but the man failed to attack. Instead, he remained at the desk, turning a small handle set into the side of the music box. A bundle of cables ran into a junction box on the wall. They'd connected it to the ampliphone system, as he'd thought.

Edward stepped closer. Still, the man turned the handle. The box relied on a wind-up mechanism. The most advanced technology in the world had been bought low by a hand-cranked device. The most heinous crimes he'd ever witnessed had been powered by clockwork. He nearly laughed, but choked it back. It would have been the launch pad for hysteria, not humor.

Even as he took aim, the creature ignored him, content to crank away like an organ grinder. Lady Holden had apparently preloaded the marionette with just one task, unwilling to chance any breakdown. Edward released the trigger, feeling sick. It would be like shooting a tame animal.

Footsteps thumped in the corridor outside.

"Edward," Charlotte said, her tone rising. "They've found us!" After peeking around the door frame, she stepped outside. "Kill it!" she yelled, firing down the corridor.

"It won't make any difference." Up close, he saw a flywheel was storing energy. It would keep transmitting until it wound down. "I've got to disconnect it!"

"Then – do it – fast," she warned, between shots. "There's too many!"

Edward examined the mechanism before realizing he was over-thinking the matter. Sledgehammer, he thought. He took aim, closed his eyes, and emptied the magazine into the casing. If it didn't work, they were dead anyway.

When he opened them, the music box was wrecked, the beautiful device reduced to a mass of walnut veneer splinters and scrap brass. The cylinder had stopped turning.

"Edward," Charlotte whispered. "Come here."

A group of marionettes stood in the corridor, as still as shop window mannequins. It might have been comical had they not frozen mid-attack. Most were armed.

"Has it worked?" she asked, still keeping her gun up.

"I think-" He closed his mouth as one of the Jills moved.

She woke from the trance, but instead of attacking, she turned and walked away. Another one followed. Looking confused, a Jack dropped the shovel he carried and set off.

"I think so," he gasped, daring to breathe again.

The two Jills at the rear of the group had obviously been tasked for cleanup duty; as the others left, they began collecting the fallen tools.

"I don't believe it," Charlotte muttered. "From killers to cleaners?"

"They're just resuming their last set task. Come on. We need to contact the Captain."

"Wait." She scowled. "We should go after Natalie."

"Agreed, but the ship comes first. Let's go."

Edward looked back into two-seventeen. Behind them, the marionette at the desk dutifully continued his work, cranking a handle connected to nothing but air.

THIRTEEN

"Sergeant, for God's sake," Charlotte shouted over the gunfire. "They're harmless now. Look!" She pointed at a Jill working in the Captain's fly quarters.

The marionette ignored them, and continued to clean up broken glass.

"I'm sure you're right, miss," he agreed, but he gunned her down nonetheless. "Can't be too careful."

To prevent any further insurrection, the soldiers were executing every marionette on the bridge. The enthusiasm with which they carried out the task suggested they were taking the opportunity to exact some revenge. Edward didn't approve, but part of him understood. They'd seen too many friends and colleagues die.

"Captain on the bridge!" The junior officer stood to attention as Fitzjames climbed up.

His presence seemed to calm the crew immediately; their training told them that so long as the chain of command was preserved, things would be alright. Edward envied them.

"Prepare interceptor two for launch," he ordered, crossing to the helm. "You! Ensign-"

"Golding, sir," the young officer supplied.

"I want a boarding squad on that boat in five minutes. See to it."

"Natalie?" Charlotte asked, as the crew rushed to execute his order.

"Gone. We arrived too late to stop her." He rested his mini-maxim against the console. The muzzle was stained black with carbon.

"The gunner will have a firing solution at any moment, sir." The ordnance officer waved a hand toward the rear of the bridge.

Behind them, the ballistic extrapolator, or 'gunner' in naval parlance, continued to grind out the calculations. The eight-foot tall array of gears and axles looked like a giant carriage clock, but could outperform an army of mathematicians. The tumblers stopped.

"We can fire on your order, sir."

Out on the forecastle, the bow turret began to turn.

"No." Staring out to sea, he shook his head. "She may have taken hostages. And I want her alive," he added. "Alive to be sentenced – assuming, of course, that any of us survive. In the unlikely event that we do, I shall be recommending to the admiralty that we withdraw marionettes from general service. We cannot be so vulnerable." He turned back. "You rendered her device inoperable?"

"Very." Edward felt a childish flash of disappointment when no response came. A 'well done' seemed to be in order. "As far as we know, it's worked. They all seem normal."

Their journey back through the ship had been surreal. The marionettes had resumed their normal functions. It was almost as if nothing had happened, but the illusion lasted only until you encountered the next bloodied corpse.

"What about engineering?" Edward enquired.

"Secured. I left them trying to rig a repair."

"How bad is it?"

"Sir," a crewman called. "Lifeboats seven through twelve are ready. Launching now."

Edward looked out over the port side. The free-fall lifeboats slipped down their rails, and splashed into the open water resulting from the *Dominator's* turn. They began to head back along the narrow ice-free channel, but their small engines afforded them only slow progress. Just as Holden had projected, they would never reach the minimum safe distance.

"Speed up the evacuation," Fitzjames said, beginning an oblique answer to Edward's question. "They can slow it down. No more."

"What about a crash shutdown?" Edward tried to bring his expertise to bear. "Could the governing rods be manually-"

"They lost five men trying."

Edward crossed to the engineering station. The temperature gauges all read zero, but he made no attempt to delude himself. The components inside the decay sanctum had melted. As he continued studying the system, a buzzer sounded. A row of lights turned red.

"Report!" Fitzjames shouted.

"No response from engineering," Golding replied, hanging up a televox receiver.

"Sound general quarters." Fitzjames picked up the ampliphone handset. After a deep breath, he gave the final order to abandon ship. "For what good it'll do," he added, after checking the transmitter was off.

"Edward?" Charlotte touched his arm.

"Hmn?" he replied, without taking his eyes from the instruments.

"Is there really nothing we can do?"

"I don't think so. I'm sorry."

"Don't be sorry. It's not your fault." She hesitated. "Can I ask you something? It might be a silly question."

"Go on." He turned around.

"Your capacitrons – they rely on water-cooling, is that right?"

"That's right." Again, disappointment reared up, although for very different reasons. He'd dared hope their final conversation might have been going somewhere more interesting.

"So that's why the ones in the launch bay didn't overload?"

"I – yes. I think it was Lady Holden that activated the extinguishers. She knew it would delay the excursion, give her time to get away." Too late, Edward saw where she was going.

"So we couldn't cool the engines the same way?"

"No." He hated himself for robbing her of hope, but lying was no use. "Charlie, the fire pumps could never deliver enough water." Using her nickname still felt lovely. He might as well enjoy it whilst he had the chance.

"That's not what I meant."

Several seconds passed before he understood. Several more passed whilst the shock subsided. He turned back to the control panel. It was a marvelously logical piece of thinking. *Could it really work?*

"Well?" she prompted.

"Captain," Edward called. "There might be a way to stall the excursion – or at least to delay it."

Fitzjames said nothing, but his expression signaled quite clearly that he expected information to be provided without dramatic pause.

"We sink the ship," Charlotte said.

"Sink her?" he gasped. His gaze shifted to Edward. "Will it work?"

"The thermal equation is extremely-"

"Yes, or no?"

"Sir, there's no way of knowing. If we flooded engineering, submerged the entire engine room, then it is possible." He looked at the lifeboats, still inching their way back up Victoria Strait. "I don't think we have much to lose, sir."

"No." Fitzjames rubbed his beard. "No, I don't suppose we do. The question is how we would do it."

"Can't you just open the seacocks?" Charlotte asked.

"Yes," he replied, with a thin smile, "but many Royal Navy architects gave great consideration to ensuring that she would not sink." He gestured around them. "We have forty-three watertight compartments. *Dominator* was designed to remain seaworthy with up to fourteen flooded, and afloat with up to thirty-two. Even if we opened every valve below the waterline, it would take days for her to sink."

"Then we'll have to breach the hull." Edward tried to calculate the volume of water needed to flood the ship, but came up with no answer better than 'a lot'.

"I can't imagine we're short of explosives," Charlotte said.

"No." Fitzjames looked out over the main guns. "We have an adequate supply."

FOURTEEN

"Surely that's enough," Charlotte panted, shoving another of the silk bags against the hull.

"Not yet." Edward called another Jack forward, took the bucket-sized powder charge from him, and added it to the pile. In an ironic role reversal, the tireless labor of the marionettes was now directed at saving them. The puppets had ferried the heavy cordite packs from the magazines more efficiently than men could have done. "What's the count, Golding?"

"Fifty-nine, sir," he replied. Unlike most of the others down here, he hadn't drawn a short straw. He'd volunteered.

"How long?"

"T-minus six minutes."

They were running out of time. The other seven locations chosen to house explosives were finished, ready to detonate. Delay was out of the question. All instrumentation for the decay engines had failed. The excursion was close.

"Start wiring them," Edward ordered.

"Sir, if there's so much as a spark-" the ordnance officer began.

"If we don't get it done, we're dead anyway." He continued packing explosives into the storeroom. Three shells had been positioned behind them, to focus the destructive energy into the hull. If his calculations were correct, the *Dominator* would be sunk by her own artillery. But if too few charges were placed, the eighteen inch-thick belt armor would hold. Too many, and they could ignite magazines all over the ship.

"Sir." He looked deeply unhappy, but began inserting detonators into the pile.

"Between the devil and the deep blue sea," a crewman remarked. He looked at the hull. "Literally."

A two-tone whistle sounded over the ampliphone.

"Emergency action message," Golding said, in between marking the count.

"Decay excursion imminent," the pre-recorded female voice warned. A corner of Edward's mind pictured the brass cylinders rolling inside the machine. On this ship, music boxes seemed to be less instruments of fun than harbingers of doom. "All passengers must evacuate immediately."

"Seventy-three, sir," Golding called, pre-empting Edward's question.

He glanced at the timer. Four minutes. It looked like an old alarm clock, but was guaranteed never to wake anyone up. Synchronized with the others, and already running, it would ensure all eight detonations took place at precisely the same moment.

"We're not going to be above decks when these go up," the ordnance officer said, still wiring the charges. "When it comes, don't cover your ears, and don't hold your breath – no matter what, you hear me? It'll rupture your lungs."

"Right." That seemed to be an excellent reason to follow his instructions. "Everyone else out," Edward snapped.

The crewmen ran, all too willing to follow that order.

"You, especially," he added, when Charlotte passed him another charge. "And be careful."

"No." She grabbed another of the silk bags. Struggling with the weight, she began to wrestle it into place.

"There's no time. Just go," he pleaded, turning back to the human chain. Last one, he thought. As he took the heavy bag from the Jill, he saw she was injured. Her face was covered in blood. More was visible through tears in her uniform. It was a miracle she was still functioning. Some indefinable feeling prompted him to glance at her face again. Recognition came just too late. The next thing he saw was the flash of a gunshot.

Edward collapsed backward.

"Hello, Doctor." With room to maneuver, Holden shouldered the carbine she'd fired from the hip.

"You!" Golding drew his pistol. Doing so saved Edward's life, and cost him his own.

Forced to deal with the immediate threat, she switched target and fired before Golding could take aim. The ensign was flung back into the charges, blood pouring from his chest.

The ordnance officer had the misfortune of being close by. Knocked off balance by Golding's body, he tried to grab his own weapon, but was already in her sights. A single shot killed him. That done, she turned back to Edward.

"Don't," she cautioned, as Charlotte eyed the gap between them. "I'll shoot him."

"If we fail, you'll die with the rest of us." Considering the pain he was in, Edward's words came more easily than he'd expected. He pressed a hand to his midriff, and found only a flesh wound. The round had ploughed a furrow through the muscle above his hip. There was a lot of blood, but no serious damage. The loose cordite all over his lap provided the answer; the bullet must have been deflected by the powder charge.

"I'll take my chances. The second interceptor will return as soon as my deception is uncovered."

"Why didn't you just go?" Charlotte asked, edging toward her.

"The damned marionettes reset as I was boarding the boat – a problem for which I imagine you are responsible." She turned the gun toward her. "I couldn't allow you to send a signal. Even if the ship was destroyed, you would have condemned me from beyond the grave. In showing you all mercy, my own good conscience betrayed me. Not this time." She nodded at the timer. "Turn it off."

"I can't," Edward groaned, feigning weakness. Obviously thinking him mortally wounded, she was now keeping the gun on Charlotte. If he played on it, an opportunity might come. "It's pre-set. And even if we could, there are still seven others."

"Very well." She turned, took aim, and fired a single shot into the timer.

Breath exploded from Edward's lungs as surely as if he'd been punched in the stomach. Still alive, still alive, an internal voice said. The damage could easily have tripped the device, and ignited the detonators. She was totally insane. Human nature compelled him to look at Charlotte, seeking eye contact. She wasn't there.

Holden fired as Charlotte launched herself off the mound of charges, but too late. The shot went wide. Again, fate was tempted, but denied; the bullet smacked into the ceiling.

Locked together, they slammed into the wall. It stunned both of them, but Lady Holden was back up first. She tried to bring the gun to bear, but Charlotte went for her eyes, raking fingernails across her face.

Edward started to get up, but his wound intervened. Under load, his torn muscle went into spasm. Groaning, he collapsed back. When he looked up, Holden had shoved Charlotte away. Blood was seeping from her left eye, but she paid it no heed, and took aim.

Edward ignored the pain, and lunged forward. Hobbled by injury, he fell short, but managed to lash out with his leg as Holden squeezed the trigger. He failed to kick the gun away, but the impact knocked the barrel high. The round intended for Charlotte's face passed over the top of her head.

Cursing, she swung the carbine around and rammed the butt into his wound. The pain was incredible; when he landed on the floor, he was scarcely able to breathe. He gasped for air, but it seemed to have little effect. His first thought was that the injury was worse than he'd realized, but this went beyond that. It was like trying to breathe in a vacuum.

As he rolled over, he put a hand into broken glass. Instinctively, he looked for the source, and both mysteries were solved. Holden's shot had smashed the lamp mounted on the wall. Gas was flooding into the corridor. They had to get out.

When he tried to get up, he saw they were all affected. They were fighting like drunks. Charlotte missed what should have been an easy blow. In avoiding it, Holden started to topple over. They went down with Charlotte on top, but Holden managed to force her down. With gravity on her side, she set about trying to strangle her.

Edward looked for the carbine, but the weapon was out of reach. Since firing it would be suicide, it was just as well. Oxygen starvation was destroying his ability to think. Scrabbling about on the floor, he found the ordnance officer's toolbox. A pry bar lay inside.

He was way past making any pretense of fair play. He struck the back of her head. It felt like a solid blow, yet she didn't go down.

She released Charlotte, and turned on him, shrieking like a lunatic.

He swung the weapon again, catching her jaw. This time, she crumpled to the floor.

"Charlotte," he gasped. "Get up." He shook her. Fear surged when she failed to respond. "Come on!"

She wheezed, trying to draw in tainted air.

"Now!" He grabbed her hands, and pulled her up. Her first deep breath provoked a coughing fit, but standing seemed to help. Her breathing settled down.

"Dead?" she croaked, looking at Holden.

"Don't know." Keeping a hand pressed into his side, he examined the wrecked timer.

"You're hurt! Let me see." She reached for his hand.

"I'm alright. It's not bad." *How long did they have?* "We need to go."

"Can't leave her." She looked around, massaging her throat.

"Are you crazy? Yes, we can."

Her eyes settled on the carbine, and Edward finally understood it wasn't mercy on her mind. She wanted to finish her.

"No!" he hissed. Although it made no difference whatsoever, instinct told him to speak quietly, as if shouting could ignite the gas. "No shooting." He pointed at the lamp. "Leave her." He grabbed her hand. "Come on."

"But we have to trigger the charges."

"When the others fire, they might go anyway." Even if they didn't, several tons of explosives were about to ignite below decks. "Leave it!"

He ran for the door, pulling her along behind. He'd lost all sense of time. *How long?*

"No!" Holden screamed.

When Edward looked back, she was aiming the carbine. Nothing happened. It was empty.

She came after them, wielding the weapon like a sword, but he slammed the door before she reached them. He wound the wheel to seal the door, straining until he could tighten it no further.

Holden thumped on the porthole before looking down. Grinning at him, she reached for the wheel. Then her grin faded, as she exerted herself. With gritted teeth, she tried once more, but she lacked the strength to open it.

"No!" Her voice was mute behind the barrier, but he could read her lips well enough.

She pounded on the glass again before stepping away. Looking down, she fumbled with something that Edward couldn't see. Then he realized she was reloading. She was going to shoot out the glass.

"Run!" he yelled. He shoved Charlotte ahead of him. "Run!"

He tried to reckon time, but failed immediately. His brain function seemed entirely devoted to controlling his feet. They covered one flight of stairs and two turns before events caught up with them.

The explosion was much quieter than he'd expected, the dense structure of the ship seeming to absorb the sound. Edward took that as a good sign. Hopefully, it meant the blast had been focused outwards.

Then he felt it. A tremor raced through the vessel, and Edward experienced the unwelcome sensation of the deck plates seeming to twist beneath his feet. The *Dominator* rocked like a dinghy crossing the wake of a larger vessel. *What forces were required to shake a hundred thousand tons of iron?*

The shock wave arrived, travelling fast. Reflected by reinforced bulkheads designed to survive heavy artillery bombardment, the expanding gases followed the path of least resistance. Inwards.

He tried to shout a warning, but too late. The displaced air struck like a solid mass, forcing the breath from his chest. The invisible force lifted them from the floor, hurling them into the wall.

Edward was too stunned to move, or even think, but humans have evolved instincts that still operate when all else fails. His began to kick in as a rumbling noise registered in his mind. More explosions?

He sat up. The rumbling continued. Had they triggered secondary blasts? No, explosions were brief. This noise was continuous. It grew louder.

"Charlotte?"

"Wassa' matter?" she mumbled, sounding half-asleep.

"Get up," Edward said, following his own orders. Aside from a mind-bending headache, he seemed intact. "Now, Charlie!" He grabbed her arm and yanked her to her feet, but she struggled to stand. She looked drugged, which was presumably linked to the huge welt near her left temple.

"You – bleed," she slurred, pointing.

He touched his ears. One hand came away sticky; he'd obviously burst his eardrum. Perhaps that explained the constant rumbling. After steadying her against the wall, Edward did something that he would later recognize as unbelievably stupid. He went back to investigate.

The stairwell was already flooded. As the churning water continued upwards, the remains of several marionettes rose to greet him. No one had thought to order them out, so they'd probably stood dumbly by as the cordite detonated. They'd been torn apart. Edward rapidly cycled through several emotions. Revulsion came first, as he looked at the human flotsam below. Satisfaction came next; his plan was working. Finally, as an extension of that, naked fear arrived, as he realized the ship was sinking. He returned to Charlotte.

"Come on!" Shoving her ahead of him, he climbed the staircase. A look at the icy water frothing beneath them seemed to dispel her confusion. Chased by the rising water, they scrambled up the stairs.

"No!" Charlotte yelled, as he started to climb the next flight. "This one stops at the service deck, remember? This way."

He couldn't remember at all, but trusted her, and followed. Behind them, water spilled out of the stairwell like an incoming tide. It was coming fast, faster than seemed possible. Skidding to a halt at the next turn, he understood why. The deck was pitching rearward. She was going down by the stern.

They beat the water to the grand staircase, but only just. Aided by their preparations, the ship was sinking fast. All the watertight doors had been left open, and unchecked, the water was filling compartments at a fearsome rate.

Charlotte lurched to the right as they began climbing the stairs. Thinking her still dazed, Edward moved to steady her, but nearly tripped over himself. Now, the *Dominator* was rolling to starboard. This had been his greatest fear; despite their plan, scuttling the ship was never going to be predictable. The equation was too complex.

"Come on!" Charlotte snapped, pulling on his hand.

Praying she wouldn't capsize, he followed.

They emerged into the arcade. The sunlight streaming through the huge observation windows was a welcome sight, but his relief turned out to be misplaced. As they ran past the shops, past the scene of that first attack – it seemed an eternity ago – the ship rolled even further to starboard. Caught off-guard, they tottered over like drunks, crashing into the tables outside the café. There was no time to be hurt. They got up and moved on, struggling to balance on the sloping deck.

To their right, the sunlight dimmed, as if clouds had darkened the sky. A rippling pattern appeared on the floor ahead of them. It might have looked pretty somewhere else. Glancing across, Edward saw the water had reached the windows. They could never hold.

Using a technique remembered from long-ago and much-hated school rugby lessons, he wrapped his arms around Charlotte's waist before allowing himself to fall. They tumbled to the ground with just enough time for him to throw himself over her.

Behind them, the mass of the water outweighed the strength of the glass. The thin barrier exploded inwards. Stained glass missiles struck home. Icy water followed a moment later. It was hard to say which hurt more.

"M– Move," Charlotte choked. "Up. Now."

Edward followed her to the stairs, splashing through water that seemed to slice at his skin. The ship had righted a little, at least. One last climb took them to the promenade deck, and the lifeboat stations. But the launch rails were empty. Their only means of escape had already sailed.

"God damn it!" Charlotte screamed. "They went without us!"

"Not their fault," he sighed. "Had to go." He'd known it was likely. When their eyes met, he saw she had, too.

"I know. But can't s – stay." Her teeth were already chattering.

He looked south, toward the bow. Although low in the water, the ship was still making headway. Knowing they would struggle to get everyone off, Fitzjames had concocted a Plan B. It appeared to be still in action.

"Let's go."

"Where?" Sounding tired, she pointed at the water pouring from the stairwell. "Can't get to castle from here."

"No. Good place. Higher." It seemed better not to waste energy on unnecessary words. "Come on."

Cutting around the higher side to port, he led her back inside. After a few wrong turns, he found the elevator he and Rupert had taken to the club. The power was out, not that he had the special key anyway. The stairwell door was locked. After appropriating a carbine from a fallen marine, he shot out the lock. A spiral staircase stood behind.

"After you." He gestured. "Exercise – do us good."

She didn't laugh, but managed to produce a smile from somewhere. Then she began to climb.

Edward waited until her back was turned before checking the wound. The exertion had opened it further, but it seemed manageable. As he began climbing, water reached the main deck.

"Is this enough?" she gasped, on reaching an observation platform.

"Hold on." He grabbed the railing, and peered down the stairwell. Water was visible at the bottom. As he watched, more steps disappeared beneath the sea. The scene had a surreal, dreamlike quality; it was as if the ship was being erased from existence. But unfortunately, it was real. "No."

They continued in silence, the water giving chase. After a few minutes, they emerged into the lounge outside the Crow's club. Edward waited a few seconds before taking a look outside. The ship had stopped. Either the turbines had failed, or she was simply too full of water to continue. Unfortunately, she hadn't stopped sinking. King William Land lay at least a mile beyond the bow, and the keel had not yet found the seabed. Their plan to beach her in shallow waters had failed.

As he looked down, the sea reached the arcade roof. The ornate glass structure gave way. Water poured down inside the ship. Instinct shouted at him to get moving, but there was nowhere left to go.

"What about the tesla dome?" she suggested. "Could we get up there?"

"Not from here," he replied, watching the sea draw closer. Below them, his workshop vanished beneath the waves. "I think we're going swimming."

"Maybe the lifeboats can still pick us up."

"Perhaps," he lied. In water so cold, they would have only a few minutes to live. She knew that, of course. With luck, those in the lifeboats could still survive. Picturing her in the water motivated him to keep trying, but he could conceive of no way out. Without hubris, he knew he was one of the best engineers of his generation, but he came up with nothing. Physics, as always, remained non-negotiable.

The ship shuddered beneath them, hard enough that Edward could swear he felt the tower sway under the force. A dull thumping sound suggested something had detonated under the water. Then the lights went out.

"What was that?" Charlotte asked.

"I'm not sure." He dared not hope. It felt like they'd hit bottom, but his over-wrought mind supplied a dozen possible explanations. A steam explosion was top of the list. He looked outside again. *Was it his imagination, or had the bow stopped sinking?* The Imperial crest on the prow was still above the waves. Even if they had struck the seabed, it wasn't over yet.

A champagne flute rolled toward the stairs as the stern settled into deeper water. Iron groaned under torsion as she rolled several degrees to starboard. Then, with one final shudder, the *Dominator* stopped moving.

Still unwilling to entertain hope, Edward looked down again. The enormous hull was gone, lost beneath the water, but a series of steel islands remained. In addition to the tesla tower, the cooling towers and masts rose skyward. More importantly, the spar decks of the fore and aft castles were still dry. Provided those aboard had kept climbing, they should be safe.

"What about the excursion?" Charlotte peered down. "Is it contained?"

"I think so." He looked at the water around the ship. It looked like steam was rising from amidships, but even the decay engines had insufficient energy to boil the entire Beaufort Sea. "I think so," he repeated. Elation overtook him. "Charlie, we did it! We actually did it!"

"Yes, we did." She smiled. "You really must learn not to be so pessimistic. "But," she said, pulling at her sodden clothes, "if rescue is twenty four hours away, we could still freeze to death. We're stuck up here."

"Hmn." He knew she was right, but he was high on victory. Her concerns seemed distant. The view outside was fascinating. All around, ice was receding as the vast heat soaked away. Making use of the open water, the lifeboats began heading back to the ship.

After a while, even the shore ahead of the bow began to thaw. Chunks of ice calved off, plunging into the water. He wondered how long it had been since Cape Felix was ice-free. Ten thousand years? Twenty thousand? And he was here to see it. Then he saw something even stranger.

Something was moving in the water near the shore, bobbing about as the ice broke up. It was a vessel, heavily damaged. She was listing to port. His first thought was that somehow one of the lifeboats had been crushed, but she was too big. And too old, he saw. The tangled mass of wood on deck suggested she'd once had masts and rigging. She was a sailing ship.

"Charlie." It came out as a whisper. Surely it couldn't be? "Charlie, look!"

Wishing for a telescope, Edward squinted at the smashed vessel. Aside from the damage, she looked to be remarkably well preserved. Her timbers were almost completely intact, although she was obviously holed below the waterline. He kept watching in the vain hope the stern might come around before realizing it was foolish; her name would scarcely be legible. Still, it was a remarkable discovery, he thought. Although their attempt to forge the passage had failed, at least they'd found some prize.

Guilt struck him. If the crippled vessel really was *Erebus* or *Terror*, then she was a ghost ship. She was a grave, and no one's prize. His thoughts came full circle. Charlotte was absolutely right: with the power off, this place could still very easily be their grave too. He finally realized she'd never answered.

"Charlie?" he repeated, turning back.

She wasn't there, but light flickered behind the velvet-lined entrance to the club. Amazingly, social conditioning was still able to exert pressure. It felt fundamentally wrong for a lady of class to go into such an establishment. Despite her apparently relaxed views on the subject, it seemed unlikely to end well. Particularly for him.

Feeling nauseous, Edward went inside. He found her gathering up candles.

"Well, I wanted an excuse to come up here," she sighed, lighting one of them. "I suppose 'be careful what you wish for' covers that."

"You did?"

"Yes. I was curious to see what depraved little games you men had devised for yourselves." She continued lighting candles. "Close the damn curtains, Edward! You're letting all the heat out. Esquimaux trick," she explained. "It only takes a few flames to keep the temperature above freezing, provided we seal it off. Is there a smaller room up here?"

"Um – the back bar," he replied, wondering how to avoid incriminating himself.

After collecting all the available candles, they retreated to the bar. He was relieved to find it deserted; this was awkward enough already. Bereft of people and music, the club seemed very different. The veneer of glamour was gone, and Edward found he didn't like what was left.

"We'll be alright in here," she judged, using the heavy curtains to block the draught. She looked at the bar. "You can even mix me a drink. I'll try to find some dry clothes."

"Ah – I'm not sure they'll have anything – suitable," he stuttered, picturing the outfits he'd seen on his first visit.

She went anyway.

He selected a bottle of scotch and poured out two glasses. Whilst she was gone, he checked his torn muscle again. He probably needed stitches, but not urgently. It did need to be cleaned. After anesthetizing himself with several mouthfuls of scotch, he put the antiseptic properties to use, and splashed liquor into the wound.

"That was interesting." She returned to the bar, and sat down. "Well, you were right."

Edward tried to gauge her reaction, but failed. He decided it was best to say nothing, and passed her a drink instead.

"They have nothing in my size." She sipped her drink. "That was a joke, Edward," she added, when he remained silent.

"You're not angry?"

"Why should I be angry with you?"

"Well, I thought that-" He stopped himself as her choice of words struck home. He'd allowed fantasy to color his perception of their relationship. She had no reason to be angry with him, for there was nothing between them. The simple truth was that he didn't matter enough for her to be upset over. "I meant that I – thought you would be offended," he said, trying to recover. "Ladies sensibilities, and all that."

"Oh, for God's sake," she snapped.

Not for the first time in life, Edward rued his inability to lie well. As if it weren't bad enough that she obviously didn't share his feelings, she looked downright angry about it.

"If we're going to spend the night together up here, we need to get some things straight, right now."

"Charlie, please," he began, trying to avoid further embarrassment. "There's really no need. I'm not so foolish as to presume that you-"

"In fact," she continued, ignoring him, "I think it's time we discussed your whole attitude."

"What?" he gasped.

"First, I don't recall actually giving you permission to call me Charlie. It's far too familiar, especially for a man of your class."

"Class?" he echoed, confounded by her abrupt change of character. Her harsh words made him realize the true depth of his feelings. They were based not on her looks, lovely as they were, but her kind nature. Had he misjudged her that badly?

"Charlotte." He took her hand. "I'm sorry if I-"

"How dare you touch me without permission?" She pulled her hand away. "Have you forgotten who I am?"

Edward tried to formulate a reply, but failed. Wounded by her attack, he seemed unable to think.

"Then there's the matter of your conduct." She stabbed a finger into his chest. "Shoving me to the ground and mounting me like some damned animal!"

Could she really be this obtuse? His only thought had been for her safety. Part of him wanted to explain. Part of him felt compelled to apologize, although he had no idea why. And another part, perhaps the part worn down by the events of the last twenty-four hours, wanted to tell her to shut the hell up.

In a rare development, his indecision turned out to be of benefit. Whilst the three elements of him did battle, she stepped forward. Smiling, she placed her hand on his chest, resting it on the spot she'd hit a moment ago.

"I should like you to do it again."

ABOUT THE AUTHOR

Daniel Durrant is a new author writing mainly in the horror and science fiction genres. His short stories have been published in anthologies in the UK and USA, and he is currently working on his first full-length novel. He lives on the Norfolk Coast in England.

5152871R00080

Printed in Great Britain
by Amazon.co.uk, Ltd.,
Marston Gate.